HER THREE PROTECTORS

The Hot Millionaires #3

Zara Chase

MENAGE EVERLASTING

Siren Publishing, Inc.
www.SirenPublishing.com

A SIREN PUBLISHING BOOK
IMPRINT: Ménage Everlasting

HER THREE PROTECTORS
Copyright © 2012 by Zara Chase

ISBN: 978-1-62241-604-2

First Printing: October 2012

Cover design by Les Byerley
All art and logo copyright © 2012 by Siren Publishing, Inc.

Printed in the U.S.A.

PUBLISHER
Siren Publishing, Inc.
www.SirenPublishing.com

HER THREE PROTECTORS

The Hot Millionaires #3

ZARA CHASE
Copyright © 2012

Chapter One

"Yes, who is it?"

Porcha pushed the button on the video entry phone, a simple task made difficult because her fingers shook so badly.

"You're expecting us."

Us? Porcha's heart crashed against her rib cage. She peered at the three figures filling the small screen, hyperventilating as panic and confusion clouded her brain. Tension and lack of sleep made it difficult to think straight. Was this for real, or could it be a clever trap? One man. She'd asked Georgio to send one man. Why would he think she needed three?

"Georgio sent us. The name's Anderson."

The speaker was at least six two, with the swarthy complexion of a South American and black hair tied back in a ponytail. As though sensing her scrutinizing him, he removed his shades and revealed intelligent dark eyes that flashed with annoyance. Clearly, he didn't appreciate being kept waiting. Too bad! Porcha wasn't about to let anyone in until she was absolutely sure they were who they said they were.

The designer stubble peppering Anderson's jaw did little to disguise his film-star looks. His aquiline features, strong jaw, and deep vertical lines in a forehead currently knotted with impatience hinted at both competence and tough resourcefulness. If he really was Georgio's man, she'd expect nothing less.

What the hell…her life was on the line, and she was wasting precious time ogling a fit-looking man. His appearance didn't mean diddly-squat. The people out to get her might have chosen a handsome man to lull her into a false sense of security, and she'd almost fallen for it. Porcha grabbed her iPad and pulled up the picture Georgio had e-mailed of the man he was sending. They *looked* one and the same, although the picture didn't do him justice.

"We're kinda conspicuous out here, Ms. Ballantine."

"I…I was only expecting one of you."

The man calling himself Anderson hitched impossibly broad shoulders. "Georgio told us all to come. We're just obeying orders."

Yes, but whose orders? "I'm not sure."

"Look, open the door. If you're worried, I'll come up on my own. Or call Georgio and get confirmation that he sent us all." Anderson glanced over his shoulder, as though he disliked hanging about in broad daylight in such a public place. "We'll wait, but not all day."

Porcha went with her instincts. Something about Anderson's expression made her feel inclined to trust him, and Porcha didn't trust easily. Just as well, or she'd have been dead by now. She hesitated for a fraction longer, came to a decision, and pushed the button to open the street door.

"Penthouse B," she said abruptly.

It would take a few minutes for the elevator to whisk them up, so Porcha made the most of the delay and sprang into action. She inserted coloured contact lenses that changed her eyes from their distinctive emerald green to a dull, forgettable gray and then covered them with thick horn-rimmed glasses containing clear lenses. Pushing her chestnut hair into a containing net, she hastily fitted on a long blonde wig and pulled a loose shirt over her tall frame, hoping it would disguise her curves. No matter what else she did to change her identity, she'd discovered with almost-fatal consequences that her assets tended to make her stand out.

Porcha had practised her transformation technique many times before and now had it down to a fine art. She checked her watch and nodded with grim satisfaction. Seventy-five seconds. Not bad.

Her hearing was acute, but there were no telltale signs of the elevator arriving yet. The doors squeaked when they opened on this floor. Porcha had made sure of that by wedging a small lump of metal in the place where they folded back—large enough to make the scrape a warning, not so big that it stopped them from opening.

She reached for her purse and extracted her S&W revolver, comforted by the feel of the grip that fitted in her hand just perfectly. Porcha hadn't had to shoot to kill, not yet, but she knew how. She'd spent hours on the range—Sal had insisted on that—and she'd had enough close shaves recently to know that she could fire at another human being without hesitation if that person was firing at her. No question about it. Her survival instincts overrode the feminine squeamishness she could no longer afford to indulge.

A sound reached her ears, and she froze behind the door, training the revolver at its centre. Boots on the stairs—three sets of them, by the sound of it. It couldn't be Georgio's men. They couldn't possibly have run up twelve flights of stairs in less time than it would have taken the elevator to get here.

Could they?

She tensed when the feet came to a halt outside her door and the bell rang.

"Ms. Ballantine, it's Anderson." *What the hell?* "Check your e-mail. I just asked Georgio to send you confirmation that we're the good guys, here at his bidding." She thought she heard him growl something rude before adding, "Seems he forgot to mention that part."

"Just a minute."

She grabbed her iPad, accessed her e-mail, and, sure enough, Georgio's confirmation blinked back at her.

"Didn't tell you I was sending you a round-the-clock bodyguard because I knew you'd say you didn't need it. You do! You can trust these guys, babe. They're the best I have, and they won't let you down. Sal would have wanted you to make use of them."

Damn right she wouldn't have asked for them, but Georgio knew the mention of Sal's name would engender complete capitulation on her part. Her training went too deep for it to be any other way. *Damn it, Georgio shouldn't have done this!* The more people who knew where and who she was, the less chance she had of coming out of this alive.

She heard the murmur of voices coming from the other side of her door, which was the last thing she needed. None of her neighbours knew she was here, but these guys could ruin everything if she didn't get them off that landing. They weren't exactly inconspicuous, but she got the impression that they *were* loyal to Georgio and would camp out on her doorstep until she opened the door, or until Georgio called them off.

She put her gun away, shot back the bolts and dead bolt, and opened the door, instinctively shielding her body with it as she ushered them in. A faint sigh of appreciation slipped past her lips as they filed past her. In spite of everything, she still appeared to possess the capacity to admire a decent male body—or rather, three of them. The spacious room seemed to shrink as they moved into it, hardly making a sound and not the slightest bit out of breath following their long jog up the stairs.

Porcha appraised her unlikely saviours as they in turn assessed her. Anderson's above-average looks when viewed through an entry phone were nothing compared to the real deal. Standing slightly in front of the other two, legs apart as though ready to move at a moment's notice, he regarded her with a combination of interest and irritation at being mucked about. She sensed power, ruthlessness, and determination in his psyche—attributes that she could put to good use if she decided to keep him around.

Anderson was wearing a tank top and cargo pants, combat boots on his feet. She got a close-up view of his torso and didn't find anything to object to in his toned musculature, bulging biceps, and trim waist. This guy spent a lot of hours keeping in shape, and she suspected his ripped body didn't result exclusively from time wasted throwing weights about in a gym. He was a man of action, and in spite of her perilous situation, she wouldn't mind being on the receiving end of the type of action he reserved for the opposite sex. It had been a while, and being constantly in fear for her life appeared to be the ultimate aphrodisiac.

"Georgio should have warned you that he'd sent us mob handed." Anderson's voice was pitched low, a hint of anger resonating in his tone, like he didn't appreciate people wasting his time.

Porcha shrugged. "Georgio is a law unto himself."

"I'm Troy Anderson." He extended a large hand, and Porcha instinctively gripped it, feeling a reaction all the way to her pussy when his long fingers closed firmly around it and held it for a protracted period. Porcha had large hands and feet to go along with her large breasts, but Troy's grasp made her right hand feel small. "Pleased to meet you."

"Er, Jean Ballantine." She flashed a brief smile. "Likewise, I think. Sorry about the less-than-enthusiastic reception. I guess I'm a bit on edge."

"Which, presumably, is why Georgio sent us." Troy shook his head. "He didn't actually enlighten us as to your precise needs."

"Me either. I still don't know why he thought I needed three of you."

"If you tell us why we're here, I'll figure it out."

"Huh-hum."

Troy turned to the cause of the interruption.

"This is Adam Cole." Troy indicated another tall hunk with blond beach-boy good looks and a body to match. Porcha's hand disappeared in his as he took his turn to put the make on her, deep blue eyes sparkling with good nature.

"Nice to meet you."

"And last but not least, this is Beck Easton."

"Damn right I'm not the least."

Beck flexed impressive biceps to prove the point. He was long haired, too. Deep brown locks curled round a resourceful face that sported soft gray eyes, a square jaw, and a beautifully shaped mouth that constantly drew her eye.

"Pleased to meet you, Beck."

Porcha shook his hand, feeling rather breathless at the invasion of her space by these testosterone-fuelled jocks. She noticed Troy glancing round, taking in the closed shades and the fact that the furniture was arranged well away from the windows. Porcha turned the dead bolt and then two other locks, observing the speaking look that Troy shared with his buddies as she made the penthouse secure.

"A beautiful lady locking me in with her," Beck said, rolling his eyes. "Didn't know it was my birthday."

Damn it, they weren't supposed to think she was beautiful! That's partly what the disguise was all about. Porcha wasn't the slightest bit vain, but she'd discovered this past week that, along with her body, her looks drew the type of attention she could well do without.

"Quit fooling about, Beck," Troy said sharply, "and give the lady a chance to tell us why we're here."

"Who's fooling?"

"How can we be of service, ma'am?"

Adam actually made her laugh when he accompanied his question with a courtly bow. It sounded unnatural, mainly because it seemed like forever since she'd had anything to laugh about. It felt good to relax her vigilance, even momentarily, and she was aware of just a little of the coiled tension trickling out of her.

"It's nothing really, which is why I'm embarrassed that Georgio sent all of you. I've lost my passport, that's all." She wasn't ready to trust them yet and said the first ridiculous thing that occurred to her, accompanying her words with a helpless flap of her hands. The scatty-female bit usually did the trick. "Georgio's an old friend and said he'd arrange for a new one so I could get home to England."

"You're British?" Beck asked.

Porcha smiled. "What gave me away?"

Beck clutched his hands dramatically over his heart. "I adore British women."

"You adore all women," Adam pointed out.

"Hey, what can I say?" Beck spread his hands and grinned boyishly. "I'm just a red-blooded male who likes to—"

"This lost passport. You couldn't go to the embassy?" Adam asked.

Porcha shook her head. "That wasn't an option."

"I don't have time for this bullshit!" Troy's angry outburst caused all heads to swivel his way. "Georgio clearly knows you personally and likes you, or he wouldn't have sent us. He's not in the habit of sending his best operatives on fools' errands." He fixed Porcha with an icy stare. "If you want our help, and something tells me that you need it rather badly, then you'd best start leveling with us."

Chapter Two

At his acerbic tone, the woman calling herself Jean Ballantine instantly lowered her gaze to the floor. She lifted it again just as quickly, but Troy didn't miss her instinctive reaction. *Well, well, who would have thought it?* This uptight, seriously frightened Brit was a player. The way she responded so automatically to a dominant male voice spoke of a very well-trained sub. Beck and Adam would have noticed, too. Beck liked to play the fool, but it was all an act. He was as sharp as the rest of them. Both of his partners were now probably as intrigued by the female they'd come to help as he was. Something about her caught Troy's attention the moment she let them into the apartment, turning his annoyance at being screwed with into a genuine desire to help her.

"Let's start with your name," Troy suggested. "That ought to be easy enough. Your real name."

The woman flashed him a defiant look. "I already told you that."

"Who or what has frightened you?" Troy softened his tone. "We can't help you if you don't tell us what we're up against."

Beck stood and glanced out the window at the park opposite, careful not to move the blind more than an inch or two. He nodded once, telling Troy that the person they'd noticed loitering there earlier was still watching the building. It was too much to assume that someone else living in this high-end apartment block was under surveillance—someone other than the petrified woman who'd done such a poor job of disguising herself. The watcher was good. So good that Troy's crew had almost missed him. They were up against fellow professionals, which told him just how urgently this woman needed to trust them.

Their client sank into the chair opposite his and dropped her head into her hands. She was teetering on the edge—scared half out of her wits. Who the hell was she? One thing was for sure, she wasn't a natural blonde. Good. Troy wasn't big on blondes. He'd put money on her not needing those hideous glasses, either. She was a beautiful woman—Beck had got that right—and her disguise…well, it simply wasn't one. There was no altering the high cheekbones that made her heart-shaped face appear so exotic, the wide mouth with full lips that cried out to be kissed, the delicate little nose that turned up ever so slightly at the end, the narrow forehead currently creased with indecision.

There was squat all she could do about those aspects of her appearance, but she'd been slightly more successful with her eyes. They were huge—almost too large for her fragile face. They turned up like a cat's at the corners and were fringed with thick lashes that definitely weren't blonde. The glasses only magnified their size and the fear lurking beneath what Troy guessed were coloured lenses.

The subject of his fascination was tall for a woman—probably five nine or ten, with not an ounce of fat on her. The baggy jeans she wore couldn't hide the length of her legs. Christ, they went on forever! The seat of those jeans flapped round her buttocks, telling him there was a cute little ass beneath all that extraneous fabric. Troy's cock stood up and took a lively interest in the proceedings. Now was definitely not the time to be entertaining such thoughts, but his prick didn't seem to have gotten the memo.

Troy lifted his gaze to her upper body, almost smiling at the inefficient job her loose shirt was doing of hiding her assets. Most people didn't realize that loose clothing gave as much away about the body it was covering as its tighter cousin did. The fabric flattened against her breasts when she moved, giving all three men a clear impression of the firm flesh contained within an outsized bra.

Jesus!

"Talk to us, love," Troy said through tightly gritted teeth. "You trust Georgio, don't you?"

She nodded. "Completely."

"We're the best he's got," Adam told her. "Troy here wasn't too pleased when he thought we were being sent on a babysitting assignment and almost turned it down. You have me to thank for our being here. I told him there had to be more to it than that."

"I'm not. I…That is—"

"Georgio never sends us out without fully briefing us first," Beck mused. "This time he told us nothing. That means he doesn't know exactly what problems you've gotten yourself involved in himself but cares enough to want you protected by the elite of the elite."

She flashed a brief smile at Beck's immodest statement, but it was gone again almost immediately. Troy reached forward, pulled the glasses from her face, and peered through the lenses. As expected, they were clear glass.

"You don't need these."

"How did you know?" She scrunched up her lovely features. "I thought they made me look rather secretarial."

"You're not a blonde, either," Troy said, avoiding her question.

"She's not?" Beck pretended to be distraught, but Troy knew he and Adam would already have reached the same conclusions he had. "I'm devastated."

"Oh, what the hell!"

The woman reached up, pulled off the wig, removed the cap beneath it, and shook out a flowing curtain of rich chestnut hair. There was a sharp intake of breath from all three men.

"The damned wig itched like hell anyway."

"I think I've gone right off blondes," Beck declared dramatically. "Chestnut's the only colour for me now."

Troy hitched a brow. "Lenses?"

"Damn, you're good."

"Much as I'd like to agree with you, we're no better than the people who're after you. You won't fool them, either."

Her head snapped up. "What makes you think I'm being pursued?"

"Oh, little things like the disguise, the fact that you won't even tell us your name, that you're scared shitless—"

"And that someone's over the road watching this block," Adam added.

"What!" She leapt from her chair. "They've found me already. I need to get out of here right now."

Troy grasped her arm and forced her back into her chair. "No one will get to you while we're here."

"Count on it," Beck added.

"But you can't be sure of that. You have no idea what they're capable of."

Troy spoke in a tone of rigid determination. "The same could be said of us."

"Trust us, angel," Beck said softly. "At least tell us your name."

"Didn't Georgio even tell you that much?"

"Nope." Adam shook his head. "Which is damned odd."

She reached for her bag at the side of the chair, extracted a small pot, and lowered her head over it. At first Troy thought she was taking medication. They he realized it was a container for the lenses she was removing from her eyes. When she completed her task and looked up, all three of them audibly gasped. Adam went one stage further and swore. The largest, greenest eyes Troy had ever seen blinked at them as their owner adjusted to the removal of the lenses. A man could possibly drown just looking into those damned emerald-green eyes with flecks of gold ringing the irises. He'd definitely go that extra mile to rid them of the sheer terror reflected in their depths.

Troy exchanged a glance with his partners, their expressions mirroring what was going through his own mind.

They were in trouble. Big trouble.

"Good." Troy somehow managed to talk in a normal voice, ignoring the raging hard-on that he didn't have a hope in hell of quelling. He didn't need to look at his buddies to guess that they'd be similarly afflicted. "That wasn't so hard, was it?" *Unlike me.* "Now, how about your name."

She took a deep breath and let it out slowly. "Porcha," she said.

"Unusual name." Adam smiled at her. "I like it."

Yeah, it was an unusual name all right, and Porcha was one beautiful woman. Uniquely so. He'd heard of that name connected to another beautiful woman. Could they be one and the same? He sure as hell hoped not, because if she was they were in deep shit.

"Tell me you're not Porcha Gonzalez," Troy pleaded.

Beck shot him a look. "Salvador Gonzalez's wife?"

"The Mexican drug lord?" Adam looked shocked, and it took a lot to shock Troy's outfit. They'd seen and done it all, and then some. "Say it ain't so."

"I'm afraid so, but I go by my maiden name of Ballantine."

Porcha held the gaze of each of them in turn. Troy wasn't sure what she read in their expressions, but it caused her to burst into tears. And Troy was betting she wasn't the type to cry easily. Troy looked at her, then at his partners, and shrugged.

"We're here now," he said aloud, answering their unspoken question.

With a deep sigh, he lifted Porcha from her chair, sat in it himself, and lowered her onto his lap.

"It's okay, babe," he said, stroking her shaking back. "We'll sort something."

"Not Sal Gonzalez's wife, we won't. Not if we wanna keep hold of our important bits and pieces," Adam warned. "He's been known to chop a man's dick off just for looking at his wife the wrong way."

Troy shrugged, aware now why Georgio hadn't told them who the client was. None of them would have come willingly if they'd known. They weren't in the business of protecting drug barons and their families, particularly not vicious bastards like Gonzalez. Georgio, the wily old fox, must have known they'd take one look at Porcha and be unable to walk away.

"Yeah, we're here," Adam said tersely in response to Troy's earlier comment. "Thing is, what are we doing here?"

"We'll get some answers before we leave," Troy said. "We owe that much to Georgio, the sneaky bastard."

"She's totally out of it," Beck said softly. "Little wonder if she's been on the run for days."

"Especially if it's Gonzalez," Adam pointed out. "Even if half of what I've heard about him is true, he'll never let her leave him."

"Well, at least we know why the place is being watched," Troy said, speaking over her loud sobs.

"Yeah, but if it's Gonzalez she's running from and he knows she's here, why not just come in and get her?"

"Good question, Beck." Troy flexed his jaw. "Once she gets it together again, I'm sure she'll feel the need to enlighten us."

"Wonder when she last slept properly," Beck mused.

"Or ate." Adam headed for the kitchen. "I'll see if there's soup or anything. Then I suggest we let her sleep for a while. We won't get any sense out of her until she can think more coherently."

"Good plan. Hey, welcome back." Troy smiled at Porcha as she sat up, wiped her nose rather inelegantly on her sleeve, and offered him a watery smile. "Sorry," she said sheepishly. "I don't usually cry over nothing."

"Seems to me your problems add up to a bit more than nothing," Beck remarked casually.

"Adam's heating up some soup for you," Troy told her. "Then you're gonna sleep."

"I can't. I need to—"

"You don't need to do anything except sleep," Beck said, serious for once. "We'll be here, and no one will get anywhere near you, I can promise you that."

"You can't be sure."

Beck flexed a brow. "Aw, come on, sweetheart. Do we look like pussycats?"

She actually giggled at that. "No, of course not. I'm sorry. I guess I got used to taking care of myself the past couple of weeks."

The men shared a glance. She'd been on the run, all alone, for two whole weeks? No wonder she was flat out of gas.

"Food up," Adam called from the kitchen.

They made her sit at the kitchen bar, watching her until she'd spooned up every last drop of Adam's chicken soup and soaked it up with the crusty bread he'd obviously found in the freezer and reheated. When she was done there was actually a little colour in her face.

"Okay. Off to bed with you."

"But don't you want to know—"

"Yeah, we do, but we need you to get some rest first."

Troy took her arm and frog-marched her down the corridor to the master bedroom. He opened the door, propelled her inside, and made sure the blinds were securely closed.

"There's no way anyone can see this window from outside," Adam said from behind him. "I already checked it out."

"Good. Okay, babe, get some rest. Yell if you need us. One of us will be right outside the door all the time."

"It doesn't seem right." She shook her head. "It's not fair—"

"Just do as you're told," Adam said. "Take it from Beck and me, when Troy makes up his mind about something, there's no point arguing with him."

When she still looked inclined to do just that, Troy laid it on the line. "You're scared silly, and there are two golden rules when you find yourself in that situation. Eat when you can and sleep when you can." Troy ticked them off on his fingers to emphasise his point. "You never know when you'll get the chance again."

"And chances don't come better wrapped than with us three to look out for you," Beck said, blowing her a kiss.

"Beck has issues with modesty," Adam told her.

Porcha smiled, her enormous eyes encompassing all three of them as she did so. "Well, all right then, perhaps I'll try and get some rest. Thank you." She briefly touched Troy's arm. "You don't know how much I appreciate what you're doing for me."

"Wouldn't mind finding out," Beck remarked as they closed the door on her.

"You realize she's a player," Adam said.

"Yeah, I got that." Troy frowned. "Gonzalez has a reputation for using her like a possession, flaunting her to help him get what he needs out of others."

Beck frowned. "He made her a slave?"

"Not sure. Perhaps she's had enough of him controlling her and is trying to get away from him."

"Then I vote that we help her," Beck said without hesitation.

"She's obviously completely traumatised by whatever's happened to her," Adam said, grimacing. "I don't like seeing her so upset, but I guess we'll find out soon enough what she's running from."

"You think if we sort out her problems, she might be persuaded to play with us?" Beck grabbed his groin and groaned at the possibility. "If you knew what thoughts—"

"We know," Troy and Adam said together.

Chapter Three

"Check out the rest of the place," Troy said.

"Already done," Adam replied. "Two more bedrooms, another bathroom, and that's about it."

"Okay." Troy consulted his watch. "It's nine o'clock. It'll be getting dark soon. We still got company outside?"

Beck took a peek. "Yep. Same guy. He hasn't moved."

"Good." Adam stretched his arms above his head and yawned. "At least we know where he is."

"I'll take first shift," Troy said. "We'll go three hours a piece. Let her get a decent rest."

"Fair enough." Beck headed for one of the spare rooms. All three of them practised what Troy had just preached to Porcha and slept wherever they happened to be, whenever an opportunity arose. An actual bed was a rare luxury. "I shall go and dream about the lovely Mrs. Gonzalez." Beck patted the bulge in his pants and sauntered off. "Do you reckon she's a screamer?" he asked, looking over his shoulder at them. "Please tell me you think she is. I do like a woman who expresses herself freely in bed."

"We know," Troy and Adam said together, giving him the finger.

"You go, too, Adam. I'll wake you in three."

Not wanting to disturb Porcha when he patrolled between the window and her door to check on the guy outside, Troy removed his boots and wriggled his liberated toes. Then he settled down in a comfortable chair, trying to figure out what this could be all about. Whatever it was, it wouldn't be good news. Anything to do with drug dealers never was, which was why Georgio never got his operatives involved in assignments that even hinted at narcotics. Troy was tempted to contact Georgio and find out what his connection to the lovely Porcha actually was but dismissed the idea. If their wily employer—purveyor of elite security services to those who could afford the best—wasn't saying, then nothing they did or said would change his mind.

An hour ticked by with no activity at all. Hopefully, Porcha was asleep. The guy in the street had been replaced by the night shift, but other than that nothing had changed.

An earth-shattering scream from Porcha's room had Troy hoisting a hand gun and hitting her door at a run. The other two emerged from their rooms a fraction of a second later, wearing boxers and also toting guns. Troy's mind whirled. He had been vigilant. No one had entered the apartment through the main door, and no one could access her room through a window twelve stories up with no fire escape close at hand. What the fuck had happened?

He barged through the door, weapon held in front of him, just as Porcha rolled from her bed and came up in a professional crouch, pointing a gun directly at him.

"Porcha, don't!"

She didn't appear to hear him. Her expression was stone-cold, her eyes glazed with determination as her finger tightened on the trigger.

"Stay where you are or I'll shoot."

"Sure."

Troy raised a nonthreatening hand—the one not holding his own gun—whilst he assessed the situation. She was going to shoot anyway. He'd seen that look in the eyes of a gunman too often to misinterpret. Unless he did something, he was seconds away from death, and Troy wasn't ready to die quite yet.

There was only one thing he could do. Without hesitation, he leapt forward, grabbed her wrist, and forced the gun free from her fingers just as she pulled the trigger. It discharged against the wall with a soft pop.

"Porcha!"

"What's the matter with her?" Adam asked.

"She's catatonic."

"That means in a trance," Adam told Beck.

"Smart-ass!"

Porcha had gone limp in Troy's arms, her eyes wide and staring at something only she could see.

"Hey, Porcha. Come back to us."

"He's here." She suddenly sprang to life, struggling to get free of Troy's grasp. "I've got to get away. He'll hurt me."

The guys shared a look, none of them knowing quite what to do. Troy shook her by the shoulders, gently at first and then more firmly when she didn't respond. Suddenly, her eyes focused again, as though she'd just woken up. She blinked several times at the three concerned faces watching her.

"What happened?"

"You almost blasted Troy's head off," Beck told her, grinning. "We owe you one. We've been trying to get someone to do that for years."

"I didn't, did I?" A hand flew to her mouth. "I can't have. I'd remember if I had?"

"It's okay, I think."

Troy extended a hand and helped her to her feet. She was wearing a tank top, with nothing beneath it, and silk boxers. All three of them gaped at the sight of her heavy nipples pushing against the thin fabric. Beck actually groaned.

"I'm sorry," she said. "I must have heard something in my sleep and reacted instinctively."

"How long have you been doing that?" Troy asked.

She shrugged. "Long enough."

"You always sleep with a gun under your pillow?"

"Doesn't everyone?"

"Go back to bed, guys," Troy said. "I've got this."

"We're good." Adam folded his arms across his chest. Beck was the talker, but Adam enjoyed the sight of a half-dressed, beautiful woman as much as the rest of them.

"Go!"

Beck picked up Porcha's gun, slipped the safety catch on, and the two of them backed out of the room, taking the weapon with them. They could be heard bitching and complaining about Troy getting all the best jobs as they made their way back to their rooms.

"Come on, sweetheart. Let's get you back to bed."

"I can't sleep." She sat on the edge of the bed and shook her head, sending tangled hair cascading all over the place. "Every time I close my eyes I think I hear something." She levelled a tormented gaze on his face. "I could have shot you!"

"Not a chance."

"But I could have. I know how."

Yeah, Troy knew she did—now. "Come on." He pulled the coverlet back. "You need your rest."

"Stay with me."

"What!"

"I can't sleep. Not on my own. I get these terrible images inside my head and—"

"Darling, don't think I don't appreciate the invitation, but I really don't think that's such a good idea."

"Why not?"

Troy rolled his eyes. No one could possibly be that dense, especially when they looked the way she did. "If I get into bed with you, we won't be doing any sleeping, and that's a guarantee."

She offered him a full-on smile. "What makes you think it's sleep I had in mind?"

"Porcha, I—" Troy stood in the middle of the room, shaking his head, feeling downright awkward. "You're married. You're scared. You want to do this for all the wrong reasons."

Her gazed travelled the length of his body, making no effort to disguise that she liked what she saw. She hadn't slept for more than an hour, but she was different now from the petrified shell of a woman who'd reluctantly let them into the apartment. There was obviously a hell of a lot more to her than met the eye. He kept thinking about the gun she'd had under the pillow and the professional way in which she sprang into action when she thought she was in danger. Even so, she was married.

To a drugs baron.

"He's dead," she said, as though reading his mind.

A thousand questions tumbled through Troy's head, but the expression in her eyes made them all disappear into the ether. It wasn't in Troy's nature to talk his way *out* of a beautiful woman's bed. She was a client, but that hadn't stopped him in the past, and it didn't look as though it would now. Call it part of the service, he told himself, coming to the only decision that had been a serious option since she'd made her request.

"Come here," he said softly.

He hadn't meant it to be a command, but she obviously took it as one and approached him with downcast eyes. He placed a finger beneath her chin and tilted her head gently upward.

"You don't have to submit to me."

She gasped. "How did you know?"

"Babe, all three of us knew the moment we walked into this place."

"But how?"

"Shush." He placed a finger against her lips. "Later."

"Don't you want to know about Sal? About what—"

"Tomorrow. You can tell us all together tomorrow after you've rested. It can wait until then." Or so he hoped. He pulled his tank top over his head and stood in front of her, allowing her eyes to devour his naked torso, almost smiling when she moistened her lower lip with her tongue. "Now, where were we?"

* * * *

Porcha fell into Troy's arms, desperate for them to close about her. She needed to feel protected by him, to lean on his strength and place her welfare in someone else's hands, however temporarily. She froze when she remembered that she'd almost shot him, petrified she'd try something else, even without a gun, if the dream gripped her again. She was trained in martial arts and could take down any one of them if they weren't expecting it. Men usually weren't because their minds were elsewhere as soon as they looked at her—a circumstance that she'd learned to use to her advantage. They saw long legs, big tits, and bigger green eyes and reckoned the package added up to a brainless bimbo. The fact that a woman could use those legs and her bare feet as lethal weapons passed most men by.

How could she tell this hard man that she needed to put the horror of the past fortnight behind her by losing herself in the erotic fantasy that had gripped her ever since her three saviours walked through her door? She couldn't, not without sounding like a complete slut, so she'd use actions instead. She needed to feel alive, in control. Hell, she needed to get laid!

She lifted her head and blew softly on his lips. Troy's reaction was volcanic. With a sharp inhalation, he dipped his head and claimed her lips in a firm kiss that told her all she needed to know about him. This guy kissed like he'd done it a lot of times before, and she wasn't complaining about his technique. His mouth was warm and mobile as his lips softened to play against hers, taunting her because he obviously liked to be in charge. She retaliated by sweeping his lips with seductive strokes of her tongue, making him groan. He immediately wrenched back control by forcing her lips apart and foraging her mouth with harsh thrusts that parodied the sex act.

God, but he was good at this!

Heat flooded her body, and her pussy leaked like a drain. The air-conditioning was turned up high, combatting the heat of the Florida night. Porcha could feel her nipples harden as they rasped against the hairs on Troy's chest through the thin silk of her top. She deliberately rubbed against him, enjoying the sensation, wishing he wouldn't treat her so gently. He knew she was a sub, which could only make him—make all three of them—doms. She wanted to kneel at his feet and take whatever punishments he deemed appropriate given her forwardness but knew that's not how it would be.

Not tonight, at any rate.

Porcha couldn't remember the last time she'd had vanilla sex, when she'd been allowed to climax when she felt like it, where she didn't have to be humiliated for hours beforehand, when she'd been fucked without a nonparticipatory audience. She wasn't sure if she even remembered how it went, but judging by the size of the erection she could feel pressing into her stomach, she'd chosen the right guy to jog her memory.

"Hey, where's the fire?" he asked, breaking the kiss and smiling at her. "Take it easy, babe. There's no rush."

Porcha felt her face suffuse with colour. She'd gotten carried away, pushing herself against him in her urgent need to find release. *What the hell?* She'd started out playing the part of the slut. She might as well go the whole hog.

"Yeah, there is."

Troy chuckled. "In that case, you're overdressed."

He pulled her top over her head and stood back to look at her.

"Wow!" A slow, sexy smile spread across his face. "You're something else. Those tits." He shook his head, his expression openly admiring. "Touch them for me, babe. Pinch those hard nipples and let me watch you getting off on it."

Too well trained to even think about declining—not that she wanted to decline—Porcha filled her hands with her breasts and did as he asked.

"Close your eyes," he said. "Throw that beautiful head back and let yourself go. Tell me how it feels."

"I feel sexy as hell because you're watching me and I think you like what you see."

"That's kinda the point. Slide one hand inside your shorts, darlin', and touch your pussy. Is it wet?"

"Soaking." She groaned. "I want you inside me, Troy."

"You'll get me, babe. Count on it."

"Can I open my eyes, master? I want to see you watching me."

"I'm not your master. Not yet." She could hear censure in his tone and wondered if she'd angered him. "Open your eyes, by all means, and see what I've got for you."

She did so and gasped. Troy had shed his pants and was fisting an erection so large, so thick, that it made her salivate. She could see thick, raised veins running its length and a drop of pre-cum oozing from its massive head. She offered him a slow, sultry smile of appreciation.

"Oh!"

"Yeah, oh. That's what you do to me. Just looking at you makes me rock hard. I've been suffering ever since I set foot in this apartment, and it's all your fault."

"Then punish me."

"No!" He shook his head, like he didn't want to go with his natural instincts. "Take your pants off."

She stepped out of them and stood in front of him, hands demurely clasped behind her back, legs slightly apart to display her waxed pussy. His gazed raked her body slowly from head to foot, and he let out a soft whistle of appreciation.

"Turn round. Let me see the rear view."

Her butt, it seemed, met with his approval as well. One large hand came down to rest on it, and he slapped her so gently that she barely felt it. What she did feel was his massive cock as he ran it up and down the crack in her ass, taunting her. Is that how he wanted to fuck her? She didn't care. Whatever worked for him. She'd do whatever he asked of her. He spun her round until she was facing him again and finally touched one of her breasts. Her skin burned where his fingers made contact with it, and she instinctively pushed herself into his hand.

"Harder. I like it hard."

"Hmm, I'll just bet you do."

He dropped his head and suckled one of her nipples, pulling the rock-hard pebble through his teeth, rasping with his tongue, moulding with his big hands.

"Your tits are too big for my hands," he said, shaking his head in what she hoped was feigned irritation. Since when did men gripe about them being too big?

"I'm sorry."

"Hey, did I say I was complaining?"

"No, but—"

"Shush."

He pushed her onto the bed and followed her down, half covering her body with his much-larger one.

"Spread your legs for me."

She opened them immediately, writhing against the crisp cotton sheets as his fingers worked their way into her slick pussy, delving deep as his thumb rubbed against her clit.

"You are ready for it, aren't you?"

She bucked against his hand. "If it's okay with you."

His chuckle was full of masculine pride. "Oh, I think I could put myself out, just this once."

Porcha wrapped her arms round his neck, attempting to pull his body over hers. It was rock solid and didn't budge an inch.

"You keep telling me I need to sleep, but that ain't gonna happen until you fuck me."

"I got that part."

Troy levered himself over her, his erection pulsating against her stomach as he parted her slick folds and once again invaded her vagina with all the fingers of one hand.

"Like that?"

"It's not what I want. I'm in pain here, Troy. Please, I'll take any punishment you deem appropriate, but just fuck me first. Get rid of the pain that's churning in my gut. Make me come for you."

Troy appeared moved by her words and dropped his head to kiss her, breaking the kiss again almost immediately.

"Shit, no condoms!"

"It's okay."

"You sure?" Troy shook his head. "I don't wanna—"

"It's more than okay. If you dare to leave this bed now, I won't be responsible for my actions."

"Yeah, but—"

"I think it only fair to warn you that I'm more woman than you could handle when I'm aroused."

Troy chuckled. "Well, in that case."

He resumed their interrupted kiss, at the same time guiding the head of his cock into her throbbing pussy. She lifted her hips to help the process along and then wrapped her legs round his waist. He sank all the way home with one long thrust, filling her completely, stretching the walls of her vagina in a way she'd forgotten was possible.

"Okay?"

"Hmm, is that the best you've got?"

He reached behind her raised ass and slapped it. "Want more, do you?"

"I want everything you can give me," she said, panting with desire. "I want it hard, and I want it now."

"Demanding little baggage, aren't you?"

He increased the pace of his thrusting, groaning as he worked his way deeper and then deeper still. It seemed she'd never been penetrated so far before, but it still wasn't enough for her. Seeming to realize it, Troy grabbed a couple of pillows and shoved them under her ass.

"Get those gorgeous legs round my neck, babe, and I'll show you what fucking's really all about."

As soon as she was in position, he really went to work on her, lunging so deep that she could feel the reaction all the way to her tailbone. Porcha felt the tension of being a fugitive drain out of her as this hunky stranger fucked her like he never intended to stop. The moment his fingers slid between them and touched her clit, she felt a climax building deep in her core. About to ask permission to let it rip, she remembered that wasn't necessary and simply went with it.

"I'm gonna come," she gasped. "Fuck me, Troy. Give it to me hard."

"I'm fucking you, baby." Sweat bathed his body, even though the temperature in the room was low. "Feel that, do you? Feel my cock ramming into your cunt. You're so slick, so tight. That's it, milk it, darlin', take what you want."

She let out a long guttural moan as she closed tight about him and the tingling sensation in her limbs became orgasmic, ripping through her like a tidal wave of intense sensation.

He was still working inside her, rock solid, when she came back to earth. His lips claimed hers in a gentle, teasing kiss as he slowed the pace and gently slapped her buttocks with one hand.

"You like being spanked?"

"Hmm, I love it."

"But not as much as you like being fucked?"

She shook her head. "Nothing beats that."

"Well, let's go for the second act." He slid out of her. "Turn over."

Porcha scampered onto her hands and knees, wondering if he'd take her ass this time. He didn't, instead sliding back into her cunt from behind, his hands claiming her dangling breasts.

"Christ, I love your tits," he said, his voice thick and gravelly. "I'd pay to see them with clamps on."

"You don't have to pay. Play your cards right and you get to see the show for free."

"What do I have to do?"

She bit down on a grin. "Lots more of the same."

He thrust into her hard from behind, and she pushed back to meet him. They settled into a harsh rhythm, both of them breathing heavily as Troy picked up the pace and simultaneously pulled Porcha's thick nipples through his fingers. She couldn't decide what she got off on more—his enormous prick driving into her or the harsh pressure of his fingers on her sensitive nipples. Whatever, she was close to climax again, but Troy gave the impression that he could keep this up all night. Where did he find such iron control?

"Troy, I can't...I need to—"

"You don't need permission. Take what you want, babe, and enjoy the ride."

He thrust harder still as he spoke, and it was enough to send her into another nerve-tingling climax. This one hit her slower but was deeper and lasted for longer. Before it died, Troy finally grunted something unintelligible, slapped her buttocks hard, and shot his load deep inside her with a series of feral moans. He ground against her backside, spasming, his breathing laboured as he finally let himself go.

They collapsed on their backs afterward, waiting for their breathing to return to normal.

"Better?" he asked, wrapping a protective arm round her shoulders and bringing her head to rest on his chest.

"Much." She nipped playfully at his neck. "Thank you."

"Think you can sleep now?"

"As long as you stay with me."

"I'm not going anywhere."

"Don't you need to know...I mean, you must have questions?"

"They can wait until tomorrow. I just need to know one thing. Do you trust us now?"

"We wouldn't have done what we just did if I didn't."

"Then we'll sort everything out tomorrow." He brushed a hand through her hair. "You do know that we're doms, don't you?"

"Yes, I know that."

"That doesn't mean you have to submit to us, but it looks like we might all be together for a while. I get the impression that whatever's going on with you, it won't be fixed overnight. If you wanted to—" He paused to drop a kiss on the top of her head. "Your choice. We'll help you whatever you decide."

"I've never been with more than one dom before."

Troy chuckled. "Baby, you don't know what you've missed. Now get some sleep. We've got a busy day tomorrow."

Chapter Four

Troy slipped out of bed just as the sun was coming up, leaving Porcha sleeping peacefully. He'd fucked her twice more after their first encounter. She refused to go to sleep unless he did, and since he was at least as keen to give his cock as she was to receive it, it was a no-brainer. Now that she was finally asleep, he tried not to disturb her as he pulled on his pants and quietly opened the door. Beck sat in a chair directly outside and raised an ironic brow at Troy's dishevelled state.

"Some people have all the luck," he grumbled. "Do you know what it does to a guy, sitting on guard duty while his mate spends the night getting laid?"

Troy chuckled. "Duty's a bitch."

"How would you know?"

Troy shrugged. "Whatever the client wants."

"Yeah, I get that part. What I don't get is why you always seem to be the one to deliver."

"Anything unusual?" Troy asked.

"Other than the noise you two were making. *Oh, Troy, fuck me harder.*" For once, Beck wasn't laughing. "What's going on, Troy, apart from the obvious?"

"We'll find out when Porcha joins us. All I can tell you is that her husband's apparently dead."

"Dead?" Adam joined them. "When?"

"We didn't get to talk about it."

"Yeah, we know." Adam rolled his eyes. "We heard your conversation all over the apartment."

Troy spread his hands. "What can I say?"

"Probably better to keep it shut," Adam advised.

"Will she play with us all?" Beck asked.

"I think so." He nodded to the door he'd just come through. Porcha stood there fully dressed, her hair damp from the shower. "We're about to find out."

"We need caffeine first." Adam, the self-appointed gourmet of the group, headed for the kitchen.

"Morning, Porcha," Beck said amiably. "Sleep well?"

She smiled radiantly at Beck. "Eventually, when the boss man let me."

"Hey who made Troy the boss?" Beck complained.

"Well, all I can say is that he sure behaved like a leader."

"He does that," Adam said from the kitchen. "We let him get away with it because we don't like to disillusion him."

Troy wondered if the other two were as astonished by the transformation in Porcha as he was. Gone was the beaten, exhausted, and terrified woman of yesterday. In her place was a sassy, kick-ass ball of energy, hungry for action and—if he read her body language right—ready to fight back. If that's what a few hours' sleep and a good shag did for her, then sex ought to be a prescription drug.

They all drifted into the kitchen, lured there by the smell of fresh coffee brewing.

"There's not much to eat," Adam complained. "Just toast."

"We only kept long-term supplies here," Porcha said. "Sorry, guys. Didn't exactly have time to stop off at the supermarket on the way."

"No problem," Beck said. "We've survived on a lot worse."

"Is that man still outside?" Porcha asked, buttering her second slice of toast and lathering it with a healthy dollop of marmalade.

"Yep."

The knowledge didn't appear to put her off her breakfast. "Why hasn't he tried to get in here?"

"Because he knows we're here," Troy told her. "He probably thinks we're employees of your late husband. They'll be waiting for us to go or for you to emerge outside. Either way, they'll move today, so we have to get out of here before they do."

"Unless we wanna hang about and find out who sent them," Adam remarked.

"I rather supposed Porcha would know that."

"Where will we go?" she asked, ducking the question.

Troy lifted a strand of her drying hair and smiled at her. "What happened? How did your husband die?"

Porcha licked her fingers clean of butter smears and sighed. So did all three men, struck by the guileless sensuality of the gesture. "We first met—"

"We'll get the life story later. Just cut to the relevant bits for now."

"Okay. He worked out of Miami. He had legitimate business premises there. Import, export."

Adam curled his lip. "Yeah, and we know what he was importing."

"We lived up the coast in Jupiter. Big house, high perimeter wall, electric gates, guards everywhere. I couldn't go out without at least two men on me. Sal was petrified that I'd get kidnapped by his enemies." She inhaled deeply, obviously getting to the business end of her story, but only hesitated fractionally. "About a month ago, Sal went to Mexico on business."

Troy elevated a brow. "You didn't go with him? I'd have thought, if he was so possessive—"

"Usually I did, yes. He hardly ever left me on my own, but this time he went with just a couple of his lieutenants. I'm not sure what was going on, but I'm pretty sure it was something big."

"A large consignment?" Beck suggested.

"Possibly, but Sal had moved away from drugs, thank God. He promised me faithfully that he would." She paused, looking at each of them in turn. "He'd got into smuggling precious stones instead."

"Fucking hell!" Adam scratched his thigh. "Bit of a departure, wasn't it?"

Porcha shook her head. "Not really. Everyone associates Sal's name with drugs, but he'd become more of a facilitator. A middleman who found buyers for certain commodities, and the other way round."

"That why he went to Mexico, do you think?"

"He'd gone to finalise the off-loading of his drugs business. He was selling up to one of his rivals."

"He kept his promise to you," Beck said.

"Yeah, sort of." She grimaced. "Anyway, about two weeks ago, he was still away, and I'd been out shopping. I had my two regular guys with me. I didn't dare to go out without them, even when Sal wasn't there. He'd know, he always knew everything I did, and I'd have paid a heavy price for defying his orders. Besides, if the guys let me go against him, they'd be in for it as well."

"A gilded cage," Beck muttered.

"Anyway, we drove up to the house, and before we even got there, I sensed something was wrong. The gates were hanging open, and I could see men with guns swarming all over the grounds. My driver simply turned the car round and hit the gas. 'No way are we taking you in there, Mrs. G.,' was what Kevin said."

"What did you do instead?" Troy asked.

"We went to a downtown hotel in Fort Lauderdale, and I tried to ring Sal but got no response. I was trying to decide what to do next when an e-mail came through on my iPhone, from Sal's e-mail address."

"Saying?" Troy prompted when her words stalled.

"Nothing." She shuddered. "It was just an attachment with a picture of Sal's dead body."

The guys shared a glance. "I know this sounds like a dumb question, but are you sure he's actually dead?"

Porcha reached for her iPad and pulled up the e-mail in question. "See for yourselves."

The three of them crowded round the screen, staring directly at a picture of a man in his fifties with a full head of salt-and-pepper hair, who might or might not have been Sal Gonzalez. Troy had only ever seen pictures of the guy, so he wouldn't know, but presumably, his wife would. He was naked, lying in a pool of blood, staring through sightless eyes at the camera.

"Well, he looks dead." Beck placed a gentle hand on Porcha's shoulder. The joker of the pack could be surprisingly sensitive at times.

"But you're not running because he's dead?" Troy guessed.

"No." Porcha rolled her shoulders, as though relieving them of a heavy weight. "Not long after that came through, I got another e-mail. It was anonymous, but it said Sal had told them before he died that I knew where the shipment was and I had three days to get it to them. They would be in touch."

"What shipment?" three male voices asked at the same time.

Porcha lifted her shoulders. "I have absolutely no idea. Sal never discussed business with me, nor would he have told them that."

"Even if he was tortured?" Troy asked gently.

"Well, I'd like to think not, but—"

"What did you do?"

Adam's question saved her from formulating a more thorough answer.

"I checked into that hotel, shopped for a few clothes, and took the precaution of visiting a safe deposit box we had in a Fort Lauderdale bank. Sal kept a load of cash there in case of emergencies, and I figured this qualified as an emergency." She sighed. "Three days later there was still no word from Sal, so I had to accept that he really was dead. I was still too scared to go home and thought I was safe in the hotel. I booked a suite with two bedrooms, and my two guys stayed with me."

"Did they try their luck?" Beck asked, scowling.

Porcha shook her head. "They knew better than that."

"Okay, babe, carry on," Troy invited.

"Two thugs turned up on the third day, knocking on the door like they were expected. When Kevin opened it, they barged past him as though he was a scrawny nobody, and Kevin, you ought to know, is built like you guys."

"What were they like?"

"South American, big, menacing, wearing dark glasses." She shrugged. "I was too stunned by their appearance to take much notice."

"Presumably, they wanted this mysterious shipment."

"Yep, but I played dumb, said I didn't have a clue what they were talking about."

"You must have been petrified," Adam said, gently touching her arm.

"I was but tried not to show it. I figured that they'd searched the house for whatever it was that was missing, and if it wasn't there, they needed me in one piece to get it for them. In that case, as long as I played for time, I wasn't going to die. I managed to establish it was diamonds they were after and said I thought I knew where they might be. I said to give me twenty-four hours."

"And then you ran," Beck surmised. "Sensible girl!"

"I didn't run because I didn't know where the diamonds are—"

"You ran because you didn't know how the guys could have found you, unless one of your bodyguards gave you up," Troy finished for her.

"Precisely."

Beck shook his head. "No wonder you didn't trust us."

"You could have been followed when you fled from the house."

"Kevin says we weren't, but if he was the grass—"

"They could have traced you other ways."

"I kept my cell phone off, didn't use credit cards."

Troy quirked a brow. "He trained you well."

"We kept this apartment here in Tampa as an emergency bolt hole. Sal thought no one would think to look for us on this side of the state. No one, not even our most-trusted guards, knew about it, so how that man outside got onto me is a mystery."

"Someone always knows about these things. Realtors, lawyers." Adam spread his hands. "And money talks."

"Yeah, well, I had a time of it getting here. I couldn't rent a car or hop on a plane to anywhere without using a credit card, so I had to try and disguise myself and ride buses."

"We need to get you out of here," Troy said. "Those guys won't hang about outside for much longer. Pack a small bag."

"How will we get past him?"

Troy got up and peered round the blinds. "It's Florida, it's the weekend, and that's a park over there." He grinned at Porcha. "Go pack that bag."

She returned a few minutes later. "Do I need the wig?"

"No, just a ball cap and shades oughta do it."

"That I can manage." She produced a cap, squished her hair beneath it, and put on glasses that covered half her face. "Just like a million other women in Florida."

"Not quite." Adam's gaze lingered on her breasts.

"Can I have my gun back?"

"Only if you promise to shoot Troy this time."

* * * *

Beck produced the S&W, watching her as she stuffed it in her purse.

"Okay, Beck," Troy said. "Let's lose our friend outside."

Grinning, Beck pulled a phone from his pocket and dialled 911.

"Oh, hello," he said. "I'm with my daughter in a downtown park." He gave the address. "There's this odd-looking man hanging round. I've seen him talk to a couple of the kids. I'm sure it's nothing to worry about, but I thought I ought to report it. You hear such terrible things nowadays."

Beck hung up without giving his name. "Two minutes, I reckon. Get ready."

"Go bring the truck to the front door," Troy said to Beck.

Sure enough, a squad car pulled up within Beck's two-minute estimate, and two officers descended on the watcher.

"Go!"

Troy led the charge down the stairs, toting Porcha's bag like it weighed nothing at all.

"Don't you guys believe in elevators?"

"Nope. There's no place to run in an elevator if things get awkward."

They burst out the front door, Adam and Troy shielding Porcha as they crossed the sidewalk and piled into a Dodge truck idling at the curb. As soon as the door closed behind them, Beck moved away in an unhurried fashion that didn't draw attention to them.

"Where are we going?" Porcha asked, her head resting in Adam's lap in the back of the cab so that she wasn't visible to anyone else who might be watching them.

"To our love pad," Adam told her, pulling the cap from her head and spreading her hair all over his thigh.

"Sorry I asked."

"Seriously, darlin', we're going to St. Pete Beach. Us gentlemen have a town house there that's more secure than Fort Knox. No one will look for you there because they don't know you're with us."

"I really do need a passport." She addressed the words to Adam's muscled thigh, trying to ignore the intriguing bulge in his pants.

"Where's yours?" Troy asked.

"At the Jupiter house, but I don't feel inclined to pop back for it."

"And if we get you one, what then?" Troy turned from the passenger seat and pinioned her with a look she found hard to interpret.

"I'll go back to England, of course."

Troy shook his head. "Baby, you think the people who have the power to get to one of the best-protected racketeers in the country won't be able to get to you there?"

She slumped against Adam's legs. "I guess."

"You can sit up now," Troy told her.

"Please don't," Adam wailed.

Laughing, Porcha levered herself upright. "What would you suggest that I do instead?"

Beck raised his hand. "Can I answer that one?"

"Beck," Adam growled.

"How about trying to find out who's chasing you and why they think you know where the stones are?"

Porcha quirked a brow. "Just like that?"

"Why not?" Troy grinned at her. "Nothing like going on the offensive if you wanna rattle a few cages."

"Yes, but where to start?"

"Presumably, you still have numbers for the two guys who protected you?"

"Yeah, but I don't know which one—"

"Call them both when we get to the house. If one of them is in on it, he'll pick up. If they both do, we'll deal with that, too."

"Okay."

Beck turned off the interstate. A short time later, he pressed a button on the dash, and the door to a subterranean garage beneath a tall waterside town house slid up.

"Welcome to our humble abode," Adam said, opening the door and helping Porcha out of the cab.

"You guys live here together?"

Beck waggled his brows. "And play."

"When we're not on assignment," Adam told her, leading the way up the stairs to a solid-looking door.

"Do you always go on assignment together?"

"A lot of the time, but not always." Adam grinned. "We both need a break from Beck every so often."

Beck glowered at his buddies. "I love you guys, too."

Adam unlocked, stood back, and allowed her to pass in front of him into a surprisingly large living area. She sensed Troy behind her as she gazed through picture windows to the intercoastal waterway immediately beyond a small yard with a boat dock. There was a fast-looking open-cockpit boat secured to it.

"Just to put you at your ease," he said, massaging her shoulders with rhythmic swirls of his large hands, "the only way into this house is through the garage or front door. Both are solid steel, and an alarm sounds if anyone so much as breathes on them the wrong way. The windows are triple glazed and bulletproof. They're also tinted, so you can see out but no one can see in."

"You must have pissed off some real bad-ass dudes," she said, feeling a little awestruck.

Adam grimaced. "Baby, you have no idea."

"It's easier to police than your big estate in Jupiter, plus we have the added advantage of being able to get out by water if necessary." Troy took her hand. "Come on, I'll show you round."

"Everywhere?" asked Adam and Beck together.

"I think she can take it."

"Then there's no way in hell she goes up there without us," Adam said.

"Go where?"

"You'll see." Beck took her other hand. "Come on."

The tour of the floor they were on didn't take long. A large open-plan living room and gourmet kitchen, full of state-of-the-art equipment, was all there was to see. The study was also equipped with the latest cyber gadgets. There was a half bath and an open-slat staircase leading to an entrance hall at the same level as the garage.

On the first floor, there were four bedrooms, all with their own facilities.

"This one's for you," Troy told her, dumping her bag on the bed in a pleasant room painted a pale shade of blue.

"Thanks." She turned to face her three eager protectors. "What is it you're not telling me?" she asked suspiciously.

"Come on," Troy said. "There's more."

Another flight of stairs led to the loft. Porcha stepped inside and gasped. The entire floor was the guys' playroom. An enormous circular bed, easily able to accommodate four people, dominated the centre of the space. The walls were covered with paraphernalia that pegged them as doms. Porcha recognized most of it and guessed the guys could tell she was excited by what she saw.

Troy sat on the edge of the bed, pulling her down on his lap. The other two sat either side of him.

"Your choice, babe," he said softly, nuzzling her neck. "But you play with one of us, you get us all."

"Three for the price of one," Beck joked. "How bad can that be?"

Adam ran a hand softly over her thigh. "You'll have to submit to us, you do know that?"

She nodded. "Yeah, I know."

"Sal didn't treat you well, did he?" Troy asked. "And now you're hesitating. You enjoyed it at first, I think, but something happened."

She let out a long sigh. "Yes, it did."

"We won't do anything to you that you won't thank us for, not if you enjoy being spanked and—"

Porcha shuddered. "I do. Believe me, I love it."

Beck groaned, touching an erection through his combat pants. "Then why—"

"I think we need to understand what went wrong between Porcha and her husband and make sure we don't make the same mistakes."

Troy ran a hand lightly down her spine. "You ready to tell us? Does it hurt to talk about it?"

"No, I want you to know."

"We want to help you get over it," Adam assured her, his hand now resting tantalizingly short of her pussy. "And, all modesty aside, we know what we're doing. Tell you what, why don't we go back downstairs, I'll cook us all a decent meal, and then we can talk about it?"

Chapter Five

Porcha watched in a trance as the three men acted as a tight team, their joshing a thin disguise for the deep friendship that sealed them as a unit. Beck volunteered to go out for supplies, taking with him a long list written in Adam's spidery scrawl.

"I need to shower," Troy said, heading for the stairs. "Won't be long."

"Can I help?" Porcha asked Adam, strolling into the kitchen area and looking round his shoulder to see what he was cooking.

"You can keep me company." He turned behind him, grabbed a bottle from the fridge, and waved it at her. "You look like a white-wine kind of gal."

"Yes, please, I could use one."

He opened it, poured her a glass, and opened a beer for himself. "You all right?" he asked. "Sorry, stupid question. Of course you're not, but we will sort this. If it's any consolation, we've been doing this a while and haven't lost a client yet."

"You guys are really close, aren't you?"

"In spite of Beck being an ass, yeah, we are. We were all in the military together, back in the day. That's how we met." He stirred something in a pot. "That's where we met Georgio as well. He was our CO."

"Oh, I didn't know."

"Well, none of us talk about those days much." He checked the oven temperature and shook his head. "Then we were all mercenaries for a while, risking our butts in various hellholes at the ass end of the world. We made enough money to quit a few years ago and now do what we do…well, because we don't know how to anything else, I guess, and because we need something to get up for in the mornings."

That was quite a speech for Adam. Porcha already had him pegged as a man of few words.

"I'm glad you do," she said, meaning it. "You make me feel safe."

"That's the general idea." He took silverware from a drawer. "How did you meet Georgio?"

"In London. I was a nurse, if you can believe it."

Adam waggled his brows. "I'll bet you cause a general rise in the male patients' collective temperatures just by walking onto a ward."

"Hardly. Georgio's wife had leukaemia."

Adam shot her a look. "I had no idea he was even married."

"Oh, he was married all right. They were devoted to one another." Porcha shook her head, filled with sadness when she thought of Maria's untimely demise. "If you could have seen them together. It was as though the rest of the world didn't exist."

"We were in Africa popping bad guys about then."

Porcha, watching Adam work with economical efficiency in his kitchen, had trouble imagining him murdering anything more vital than a soufflé and told him so.

"You're really at home in a kitchen."

"I should be. My folks have a string of them back in Philly. I could cook before I could walk. I always intended to go into the business myself but—"

"But you got a taste for what you do now and prefer it that way."

He stopped what he was doing and dropped a kiss on the top of her head. "Yeah, I guess. We get on so well that it would be like cutting off my own arm if I left the guys." He grinned. "Besides, someone has to make sure they eat right."

"What do the others do whilst you're taking care of their nutritional needs?"

"Beck can make anything with an engine talk to him." He laughed. "That truck we brought you back in looks like millions of others on the road, because we want it to blend in. But under the hood it's a whole different story. It can outrun just about anything on the road if need be. Don't tell him I told you this, but Beck's a top-notch driver who could give a lot of professionals a run for their money."

"And Troy?"

"All those gadgets in the study. He's the cyber prince. Keeps all our communications up to date, amongst other things."

"Yes." Porcha smiled. "I can imagine him being at home doing all that stuff. He's a bit of a control freak, isn't he?"

"We all are, babe. Goes with the territory." He turned his attention back to his cooking. "You were telling me about Georgio and his wife."

"Well, he brought his Maria to London because the best specialist in the world at the time was based there. I looked after her in the private clinic he checked her into, and we hit it off from the word *go*. So, when Georgio brought her back to the States, knowing she didn't have much time left, he asked me to come, too, as her private nurse." Porcha paused to take a sip of her wine. "I was in a bit of a rut at the time. I couldn't shake off a persistent bloke who wouldn't accept our relationship was going nowhere, and so I decided a trip to the States was just what I needed."

"How long did Maria last?"

"Six months."

"We wondered why he got out of the mercenary business and came on home." Adam sighed. "He should have told us."

"He probably didn't want to distract you."

"Yeah, that would be it. Anyway, at least he set up his security business and we had something to come home to."

"My relationship with Georgio was never sexual, in case you're wondering. More father and daughter, I guess, but I know a lot of people thought there was more to it than that. He wanted me to stay on with him after Maria went, but I couldn't do that. There was a big wide world out there, I was only twenty-two—"

"How long ago was this?"

"Just over three years. Anyway, I fancied Mexico. Georgio knew someone with a club down there, a respectable nightclub if that's not a misnomer. He got me a job as a hostess, meeting and greeting the punters."

"And let me guess," said a voice from the doorway, "that's where you met your husband."

They both turned to see Troy standing there, unsure how long he'd been listening. He was wearing long shorts, a clean shirt, and was freshly shaved. Adam tossed him a beer, which he caught one-handed, and he popped the tab.

"Yes, that's where I met Sal."

"Save the rest of it until Beck gets back," Troy advised. "He shouldn't be long."

They heard his key in the door at that moment, and he staggered in, loaded down with supermarket bags. The guys decanted his purchases and stacked everything neatly in the cupboards. Shortly after that, they sat to eat the meal Adam had produced remarkably quickly. It was really good, and Porcha told him so.

"Ah, some appreciation for my talents at last!"

"You seem to have regained your appetite," Beck said, laughing at her empty plate. "What happened to the shit-scared woman we met this time yesterday?"

She grinned at each of them in turn. "She got some sleep, she got laid, and now she's just mad as hell, thirsting for revenge."

"Atagirl!" Beck said for them all.

"Where did you learn to handle a gun?" Troy asked.

"Same place I learned self-defence. Sal insisted. I spent hours on the range until I hit the centre of the target every time. I spent even more hours taking private karate lessons." She shared another grin between them all. "Just so you know, I can handle myself, so don't hack me off."

"Ah, baby, I'm sure you can," Beck said, fluttering his brows. "But can you handle us?"

The guys stood up and cleared the plates away, their movements swift and economical, always seeming to know where the others were. Porcha watched them in admiration, feeling safe and cherished. She knew she was about to tell them everything—all the intimate details of her humiliation at Sal's hands—sensing it was the right thing to do. Sal was dead. He couldn't come back and chastise her for anything. Even he couldn't control her thoughts from beyond the grave. She was free of him, and once she got rid of the people trying to chase her down, she'd be able to do whatever she damn well pleased. She was probably a wealthy woman, at least on paper, but she wouldn't take a penny of Sal's illicitly obtained funds. If she came out of this thing alive, she'd give it all to charity and start again with a clean sheet.

"Come on." Beck took her arm. "Let's go get comfortable, and you can tell us your life story."

Porcha accepted another glass of wine and curled her feet beneath her in a swivel chair. The three guys sat opposite her, all in a line on a large couch, rather as though they'd agreed without the need for any words not to touch her until they were sure she was comfortable with it. Adam succinctly brought Beck up to speed on what she'd so far told them. He, too, expressed his surprise at the news of Georgio's wife.

"He didn't tell me about any of you, either," she said. "Georgio only doles out information on a need-to-know basis."

"So, you met Sal at the club you worked at," Troy prompted.

"Yes, he swept me off my feet, to be honest. He was charming, well connected, and a perfect gentleman. He showered me with gifts, took me on his gin palace of a yacht, flew me to Rio in a private jet." She lifted her shoulders. "It was a first-class ride every step of the way. What girl wouldn't be impressed?"

"Did you know what he was?" Adam asked.

"Not at first, but his permanent protection squad told he was no Boy Scout. That and the fact that everyone treated him with grovelling respect. Georgio went crazy when I told him I was seeing Sal. He put me straight on his profession and told me to back off."

"And did you?" Troy asked.

"I tried to, which was when I discovered that no one walks away from Sal Gonzalez unless he's ready to let them go. He besieged me, launched an out-and-out charm campaign, introduced me to all sorts of legitimate business contacts and promised me he would get out of the drugs business permanently if that's what it would take to keep me. In the end, he convinced me he was a reformed character."

"Leopards don't change their spots," Beck said, unusually sombrely for him.

"No, obviously not." She groaned at her own naïveté. "But perhaps I wanted to believe it was possible because I was a little in love with him." She shrugged. "Who knows? He told me about his childhood. He came from an impoverished background, and all the kids, according to him, got involved in drugs in some way. He came up through the ranks, had natural leadership qualities, and it went from there."

"That part's probably true," Troy said.

"You're not Mexican?"

"No, I come from Argentina originally, but I know life can be as tough in Mexico as it was in South America."

"I'd been having a tough time supporting myself," Porcha said, feeling the need to continue justifying her decision to marry a man like Sal, "and it was nice to have someone I kind of trusted to make decisions for me. Anyway, I eventually agreed to live with him, which is when the fun and games started."

Adam frowned. "You didn't know he was a dom?"

"Call me sheltered, but I didn't even know what a dom was. What I did know, once he had me behind the walls of his fortress in Mexico, was that there was no going back, so I made the best of it. He trained me for weeks before he laid a finger on me, which drove me insane." The guys shared a glance. "I like hard physical sex, and I wasn't getting it, you see."

"He had you pegged," Beck said, curling his upper lip. "Knew exactly how to turn you into what he wanted you to be."

"He taught me to assume a subservient position whenever he walked into a room alone. In the end, it became second nature, even when we had company. He regularly spanked me and taught me to wait for the pain to transmute to pleasure. He introduced me to all his toys but wouldn't fuck me until I agreed to marry him." She looked at each of them in turn. "By then I was in a permanent state of arousal and would have married his grandfather if it had got me laid."

"He was controlling you from the get-go," Troy told her, anger in his tone.

"Yeah, I know that now. On our wedding night he kept me up, literally all night. He made me sit at the dinner table with nothing on except nipple clamps and a plug up my butt. Then he took me to a room I'd never been in before. Like your one, except it had a real creepy feel to it, like people who'd been in there before me hadn't enjoyed the experience."

"I hope you didn't get those sorts of vibes from our room," Adam said earnestly.

"No, I didn't."

"Good," Beck said. "Because we're not into cruelty."

"Sal chained me to the wall on our wedding night and made me turn to face it with my butt in the air. That was his favourite way to look at me, I later discovered. He finally fucked me from behind, telling me over and over again that I was his and would never do a single thing for the rest of my life without his approval."

"Was it good? Beck asked. "The sex, I mean."

"I loved it. He was thirty years older than me but still a passionate man with a big cock. Not as big as Troy's," she said, giggling, "but still pretty impressive. He filled me with it and made it last forever. I came twice without his permission and got punished harshly for it."

"Doesn't sound so very bad," Beck remarked. "Not if you liked it."

"He released the chain from the wall afterward, attached it to the collar he'd put round my neck, and made me crawl across the floor to him and beg for more."

"Did you?" Adam massaged an impressive-looking erection through his pants.

"Oh yes, and he spanked me for asking. Said girls who asked didn't get."

Troy shifted his position, also rigidly erect, Porcha noticed. "Babe, if you enjoyed it so much, and you obviously did, what went wrong?"

She shrugged. "I guess I'm not cut out to be a slave. I'm happy to submit, beg for what I want, and take any punishments my dom thinks appropriate, but outside of that I want to be able to live my own life, make decisions for myself."

"You'll give your body and not your mind, which makes you a sub not a slave," Beck told her. "That's what we're in the market for, in case you're wondering. We'd never do anything to you that you didn't want. There's always a safety word in our games."

"To answer your question, Troy, what went wrong is that Sal is a show-off. He didn't want anyone else to touch me, but he did want people to see what power he had over me. It got to the stage where he'd have one of his men in the room when he was fucking me, usually that prig Woollard."

"Woollard?"

"Let her finish," Troy said, talking over Adam's interruption.

"He was Sal's right-hand man, and we hated each other. He disliked me because he thought I lessened his influence with Sal but still lusted after me. I disliked him because he was highly dislikeable."

"He made his man watch you?" Adam grimaced. "What a sick fuck."

"Not just Woollard. My two bodyguards were regular spectators, too. Sometimes he'd get one of them to administer his punishments for him whilst he sat and watched. They were never allowed to lay a finger on me with their bare hands. It was always a paddle or a whip. I was totally humiliated because I could see how turned-on they were, but that was rather the point. But, as I said, Woollard was the worst. He used to spank me really hard with one hand and jerk off with the other. He was the only one allowed to do that. But it was the smug satisfaction in his eye that got to me. Sal knew I hated what they did to me, but I couldn't do anything about it. He'd worked his way inside my head and had complete control." She spread her hands, trying to make them understand what it was like. "And in spite of everything, I still enjoyed the sex, even if I didn't enjoy the humiliation."

"And yet Sal taught you to protect yourself—"

"Oh yes, he loved me and was kind to me in a perverse sort of way when it wasn't about sex and domination. It was just…well, this'll sound like boasting, and trust me, it isn't. He saw how men looked at me and used me as a weapon to show them how invincible he was." Porcha sighed. "The trouble was that he trained me too well for me to even think about protesting. I knew I had to do whatever he asked of me, no matter how degrading. He stripped me of the will to do anything of my own volition."

"Mind games." Troy spat the words, giving Porcha the impression that if her husband hadn't already been dead, Troy would have been happy to help him on his way to the next world.

"It got worse. He started inviting his male business colleagues to dinner and made me wear completely see-through clothing. He made me sit at the foot of the table with my tits on open display whilst they chatted like I wasn't there."

"The perverted bastard!" Beck growled.

"Inevitably, at some stage he'd say I'd displeased him, which was my sign to get up and crouch in the corner." Tears seeped from the corners of her eyes. "He didn't have to say a word. Just one look and I knew what I had to do."

"He had you the moment he didn't fuck you at the beginning, and he knew it," Troy said. "He was thirty years older than you so he needed his rivals and friends to see that you weren't with him for his money. I'm betting that you smiled all through those humiliations. Am I right?"

She lowered her gaze and nodded. "Yes."

Adam scowled. "Don't you dare say you're sorry he's dead!"

"I'm not, but the brutal truth is that if he walked in here now, I'd go with him, without question, even though I'd ten times rather stay with the three of you." She shrugged. "I just don't seem to have any will of my own when he's around."

"He knew he had to conquer your mind first, and he did a pretty good job of it," Troy said, grimacing.

She looked at the three of them, conscious of the tears now trailing down her face. "I love being a sub. I've thought about your proposition and want to submit to the three of you," she said earnestly. "You have no idea how much. Just don't humiliate me like he did. That's all I ask."

"Baby," Beck said. "There are three massive cocks here ready to keep you happy for the rest of your days. We don't need to humiliate you to get our rocks off."

"Are you ready to let us fuck you?" Adam asked. He unzipped and showed her what he was packing. She gasped. "Yeah, you want that, don't you, sugar?"

"Yes, master."

"Stand up and take your clothes off, Porcha," Beck ordered. "Slowly now. Make us wait to see what you've got for us."

She smiled, lowered her head, and then immediately stood up. When she saw the men exchange a satisfied smile she knew she'd made the right decision. They would treat her right without trying to control all aspects of her life. She pulled her top from the waistband of her jeans and threw it over her head. Beck caught it and grinned at her. Then she unsnapped her jeans and pulled them low enough for them to be able to see the thong that matched her lacy bra.

"Are you wet, Porcha?" Adam asked.

"Yes, master. You guys have really turned me on."

"You know what that means, don't you?"

"How will you punish me?"

"You'll find out soon enough. Now the bra."

Porcha unfastened it and threw it aside. Her three guys all made grunting sounds of approval when her breasts sprang free.

"The thong," Adam said. "It looks kinda damp. You might feel more comfortable without it."

She stepped out of it without hesitation and then assumed the submissive pose she'd been taught, awaiting their next order.

"I don't know about you, boys," Adam said, standing up and stepping out of his pants, "but I think this little sub of ours has been a bad girl and needs a good spanking."

"Not to mention a good fucking," Troy said.

"Couldn't agree more." Beck walked up to her and weighted one of her breasts in both hands, tweaking the solid nipple painfully and making her groan. "Come on, Porcha, it's playtime."

"At last," she said, sharing a radiant smile with the three of them.

Chapter Six

"Let's show you how much fun it can be to share."

A naked Adam swept Porcha into his arms and headed for the stairs. He could tell by the look that passed between Troy and Beck that he'd surprised them with his out-of-character behavior. He was as into the life as his buddies but wasn't usually the impulsive one. That mantle fell to Beck. But the moment Adam laid eyes on Porcha, something inside him changed. Not just because she was beautiful, stacked, and sexy as hell. The three of them had a reputation as babe magnets, and she was far from the first woman to cross his path who fitted that description. Perhaps it was her determination to take care of herself, her unwillingness to be chained to a man who wanted to control her absolutely, that inspired his admiration.

Then again, it might just be her lovely British accent that did it for him.

It was more than admiration that he felt for the feisty bundle cradled against his chest as he strode up the stairs three at a time, his cock so rigid that it was almost painful. He glanced into her beautiful catlike eyes as she wrapped her arms around his neck and kissed it. He cared about her in a way he'd never cared about any of the women he'd played with in the past, and he hadn't even fucked her yet.

Adam had absolutely no idea what was happening to him, but as her kisses turned into playful nips, he gave up trying to figure it out. Right now he had more urgent business to attend to.

Beck and Troy followed behind him, both still fully clothed. Adam knew they'd be as aroused as he was, so that situation wouldn't remain for long. Even so, he intended to call the shots this time, and Beck had better not try and take over.

Adam kicked open the door to the playroom and deposited Porcha on the bed.

"What do you have in mind for our new playmate?" Beck asked as he shed his clothes.

"Well, for starters, I think she deserves a good spanking for creaming her panties."

Adam sat on the edge of the bed and beckoned to Porcha. "Come and kneel down here."

She scampered across the bed and fell at his feet, hair obscuring her features, and she dipped her head and waited for his next command. Beck was sitting on the bed, erect and good to go. Troy surprised Adam by remaining clothed and plonking himself down in a chair where he could watch the show.

"You're in charge, buddy," he said when Adam threw him a questioning look. "I can wait."

"He *has* already dipped his wick," Beck pointed out.

"Are you sorry for what you did, Porcha?" Adam asked.

"Yes, master. Very sorry."

"Suck it while I spank you. And don't forget, any time you need to stop, just say the word."

"What is the word?" she asked.

"How about *time-out*?"

"That's two words."

"Still, it'll do the trick."

He nudged his head into her mouth, and her sweet lips closed greedily round it. Adam closed his eyes and groaned, too damned close for comfort. Her ass rose in the air as she leaned forward to take him in her mouth, and Adam brought his hand down across the tight globes. She winced but gamely sucked him deeper as he repeated the process.

"You've got juices running down your legs, babe," he told her. "That's really bad." He spanked her a little harder. "Stop sucking my cock and rub it between your tits instead."

She pushed her huge breasts together and closed them tightly round his engorged cock. Then she moved her body so that his prick was captured tightly between them one moment, its head emerging and leaking pre-cum above her nipples the next.

"Christ!" Beck had moved forward to get a closer view. "A guy could die happy after an experience like that."

Troy said nothing. He merely sat where he was, watching the proceedings.

"Get me some lube," Adam said to Beck.

"Does she need it?"

"Best be sure."

Beck returned with a tube. Adam stopped spanking her and squirted a generous amount over her backside as she remained crouched at his feet.

"You see, babe, crouching with your ass in the air doesn't have to be demeaning."

"No," she said breathlessly. "Your way I like."

Adam chuckled. "That's because you've got three men watching you, all with massive erections that you're gonna be on the receiving end of before you know it."

"If that's what would please you gentlemen."

"Oh, you'll please us all right, in ways you've probably never even imagined possible."

Adam's slick fingers circled her anus, and one slid smoothly inside. He met no resistance at all, not even a slight tensing. Instead, she pushed against him, anxious for more. He slapped her thigh.

"Did I say you could move?"

"Sorry, but I really like that."

"Go sit on the bed and rest your back against the headboard."

She scampered into position, her face flushed with excitement. Troy had finally stood up to take his clothes off. *Game on!* Adam rummaged in a drawer and found what he was looking for. He moved across to Porcha and ordered her onto her side. As soon as she moved, he inserted a butt plug and set it to a low vibration.

"Like that?"

"Yes, sir."

"Spread your legs and bend your knees up."

Beck threw him a large vibrator, and Adam eased it into her cunt. She absorbed the entire damn thing quicker than blinking.

"She's pretty desperate," Adam said to Troy. "You couldn't have done that good a job with her last night."

"Oh, I don't think she was complaining. I guess it's the thought of the three of us taking her together that's got her all steamed up."

They sat together at the foot of the bed, watching her face as the vibrator did its work. She closed her eyes and rubbed her thighs together, close to orgasm.

"You're not to come, Porcha," Adam said in a stern tone. "We've got plenty of cock here between us that'll do the job a damned sight better than a plastic toy."

"But when—"

"When I say it's time." Adam stood and grasped his cock by its base. The other two stood with him and adopted a similar pose. "Look what we have for you."

She opened her eyes very wide and then blinked, licking her lower lip repeatedly as the enormity—literally—of what she'd agreed to do stood to attention right in front of her eyes.

"Like what you see?" Adam asked.

"How did I get to be so lucky?"

"Well, now, I guess that's just one of life's odd little curve balls."

"I *don't* have curved balls," Beck protested, making them all laugh.

Adam was still chuckling when he joined her on one side of the bed and bent his head to suck and nip at a large nipple. Beck took up a position on her opposite side and did the same thing. It took both of Adam's large hands to encompass the full swell of her breast. His fingers sank into the firm flesh as his lips and teeth paid homage to its solid peak. She writhed, their combined tongues and the power of the vibrators driving her wild.

The bed sank as Troy joined them and abruptly whipped the vibrator from her cunt.

"The sneaky little madam was about to get off while your attention was elsewhere."

Adam and Beck released her breasts, ignoring her soft moans of protest. Adam removed the plug from her butt.

"Naughty!" he said, waving a finger beneath her nose. "Turn over."

She scrambled onto her hands and knees, and Adam brought the paddle Beck handed to him down hard over her buttocks. She thrashed her head from side to side, mewing with need as Adam increased the pressure of his whacks. She hadn't exaggerated when she said she liked it hard and rough, and Adam and his buddies were just the guys to deliver.

"What do you say?"

"Sorry, master, but I'm so damned hot." She did that thing with her hair again, tossing it over her shoulder in time with his spanks. "Please, I need to—"

"You never ask!" He spanked her harder, the sound of the paddle coming down on her soft flesh echoing round the loft like gunfire. "That's it, babe," he said, when she cried aloud. "Make as much noise as you like. Feel free to express yourself. We wanna know what you're feeling. This loft is soundproofed, so no one but us is gonna hear you. Tell us where you feel it."

"In my pussy. It's red hot and won't stop leaking."

"That we can do something about."

Beck grinned, dropped his head, and started to lap at her thighs.

"Oh God!" She pushed herself against his tongue. "That feels incredible. I'm ready to be fucked when you decide it's time. I want you all inside me. I want everything you can give me and then some."

The three guys all chuckled. "I'll just bet you do."

"Go lay flat on the bed, your arms above your head," Adam ordered.

She scampered into position, and Beck fastened fluffy restraints on her wrists.

"On your knees," he said next. "The restraints will swivel with you."

She did as he asked, and they took a moment to admire the view. Her cute butt, slightly red from Adam's punishments, poked skyward, her arms stretched in front of her, held up by the restraints, and her huge tits swinging beneath her elicited groans of approval from three very randy guys.

"Roll onto your side, babe. We're gonna fuck you now."

As soon as she was in place, Beck joined her, running his fingers down her tits as he got into position, and slid his cock playfully between her thighs, waiting for Adam to take up a position behind. The two guys nodded and slid into her at the same time. Beck went straight for it, ramming himself all the way home, issuing an elongated sigh when his entire cock was gobbled up by her pussy. Adam eased himself more carefully into her ass, concerned that he might be too big for her. He discovered that his caution was misplaced when she pushed back impatiently and he sank a little deeper. One more thrust and she had him all.

Troy joined the party, kneeling by her head and slipping his length between her lips. And they were away. Moving with the same precision that guided their military manoeuvres, they operated as one smoothly oiled machine, keeping perfect pace with one another.

"Christ, she's tight!" Beck's voice was an agonized moan. "She's gripping my cock like she wants to take it hostage."

"She's sucking mine like she hasn't eaten for years." Troy rammed it toward the back of her throat. "That's it, baby, take it all." He groaned. "Fuck, she's good at this!"

"I've never fucked an ass that held me so snug." Adam increased the pace of his thrusts, and the others picked up to stay with him. "That's it, babe. Milk it. Make me cream your ass with my cum. Jesus, this is heaven!"

Porcha, her hands restrained and her mouth occupied with Troy's prick, appeared to be enjoying it as much as they were.

"She's gonna come any minute," Beck warned. "She's just closed her walls round me, and it's pure heaven."

Porcha's body went into wild spasm, but she gamely clung to Troy's prick as she rode her climax and drove all three guys over the edge at the same time, something that never usually happened. They held contests when they fucked like this to see who could last longest. Troy almost always won. Beck always lost. Today they were all losers. One green-eyed siren had got the better of them all.

"That's it, babe, swallow it all!" Troy held the base of his cock, rubbing it a few times as he shot his load into the back of her throat. "See how much I've got for you."

"Here it is!" Beck said at the same time. "I'm gonna fill your cunt, Porcha." He rammed himself into her, yelling as release gripped him. "Here you go, babe, take it all and let me fuck you senseless."

"Me as well." Adam's entire body pulsated as he shot his load deep into her ass. "Geez, that's so damned good. It's never fucking ending."

Porcha, her mouth now relieved of Troy's prick, screamed at them to keep going as she came a second time. Beck, already spent, agitated her clit, slipped his fingers into her sticky entrance, and slapped her thigh, grinning as she rode his hand like a woman on a mission.

"Unbelievable," Beck said, flopping on his back, temporarily fucked out.

"Unique," agreed Troy, releasing her hands and bending over Porcha's face to offer her a deep kiss.

"Never known anything like it." Adam withdrew from her ass, patted it gently, and joined his buddies in the recovery position.

* * * *

It was Beck who got up and ran a bath for them in the huge en suite. The other two remained where they were, one on either side of Porcha.

"You okay?" Troy asked her.

Porcha didn't have to think about her reply. "More than okay," she said, laying a possessive hand on each of their chests. "That was unlike anything I've ever experienced before. Thank you."

Troy and Adam roared with laughter.

"What's so funny?"

"You are." Troy gently massaged one of her breasts. "You sound like a school teacher, all prim and proper, thanking a student for turning in a good assignment."

"Instead of which," Adam added, "you've just taken three huge cocks in various parts of your body, given us the ride of our lives, and *you're* thanking *us.*"

"We didn't make you feel humiliated?" Troy asked anxiously. "If there's ever anything we do that you don't like, you have but to say the word *outtake.*"

"No, you made me feel sexy, loved, and wanted, but never humiliated, except in a nice way." She lifted her head and grinned at them both. "I love taking orders from dominant men with cocks the sizes of yours."

"Well, in that case, you've come to the right place, so to speak."

"Bath's ready."

"Okay, ma'am, let's get you cleaned up."

Porcha sank into the warm, fragrant bubbles with a contented sigh and allowed her three hunks to wash her all over. Their hands were everywhere, and she welcomed their intrusion with a hunger that wasn't in danger of being satisfied any time soon. This was a thousand times different from the way she'd felt with Sal. He wanted to emphasise his control over her by humiliation. These guys just wanted to fuck her, giving at least as much pleasure as they received.

"Can we do that again right away?" she asked.

"No!"

Troy's answered was definitive. In spite of Beck's assertion that they didn't have a leader, when Troy said she'd had enough after taking all three of them for the first time, none of the others argued.

Beck wrapped her in a fluffy towel and carried her down the stairs to the room that had been assigned to her. It seemed she wouldn't be allowed to walk anywhere when they were playing their games with her. Still, who was she to complain? Each of them had a torso that would make even the most dedicated bodybuilder sit up and take notice. How bad could it be to get up close and personal with each one of them?

Once they reached her room, the other two guys following along, Beck removed the towel whilst Adam pulled back the covers.

"You get to sleep on your own tonight," Troy said, brushing the hair from her forehead when Beck placed her between the sheets. "That's because you need to get some rest. But after this, one or two of us will join you for some or all of the nights. We'll work something out between us. If all three of us decide to play then we go upstairs. That all right with you?"

She raised her arms and wrapped them round Troy's neck. "Stay with me now. I'm horny again."

The guys exchanged an amused glance. "So are we, babe, but anticipation is half the fun."

"Anticipation sucks!"

"So do you," Troy said, kissing her. "Damned well, too. I'm betting these two can't wait to find out just how well."

"Damned right," Beck agreed.

"They don't have to wait."

"Don't argue with your masters," Troy said, tapping her thigh through the covers. "When it comes to fucking, we call the shots."

"Hmm." She wriggled down beneath the covers. "You shoot good and deep, too. Oh well, if you won't help me out."

With a dramatic flourish, she threw the covers back, spread her legs, bent her knees, and went to work with her fingers. All three guys groaned as they watched her sink them deep inside her waxed pussy and ride against them.

"You realize," Troy said, his voice thick and hungry, "that this will get you punished."

She blew him a kiss. "That's the general idea."

"What are you think about while you finger fuck?" Beck asked.

"I'm thinking about the feel of your fat cock inside my cunt," she responded, increasing the pace of her fingers. "I'm thinking about Adam's shaft ramming into my ass, and I'm savouring the taste of Troy's gorgeous prick fucking my mouth."

"Jesus!" Beck ran a hand through his tousled hair. "What have we got ourselves here?"

"I'm real close to coming, guys. Sure one of you doesn't want to help me out here? I really like having my pussy sucked, just so you know." She glanced at them, all still naked, all three of them with massive cocks standing rigidly to attention. It was a sign of their discipline that when Troy shook his head, no one moved. "Okay, suit yourselves." Her entire hand disappeared inside her pussy and her hips rotated against it at a frenetic pace. "Here it comes. Arghhhh! Geez, that feels good."

Porcha's body stilled when the tremors finally ceased. She removed her hand and waved it in the air. "Anyone want to taste me?"

Beck groaned but manfully resisted the temptation.

"Go to sleep!" Troy pulled the covers right up over her. "We'll talk about your punishment tomorrow."

"Good night," she said sweetly, turning on her side and offering them a sultry smile. "I get the impression that I shall sleep a whole lot better than you three."

"Damned right," Beck grumbled as they closed the door on her. "Since when did a sub get to run the show?"

"Since the lovely Porcha came into our lives," she heard Troy say. "I don't know about you guys, but no matter how disobedient she becomes, I'm not about to evict her from it any time soon."

"Me neither," Adam said. "There's just something about her."

"Yeah," Beck agreed, their voices fading as they made for their own rooms. "She's more than enough for me."

Chapter Seven

Beck was alone in the living room when Porcha emerged the following morning. She was wearing a tight pair of white shorts and a pretty pink top. Beck wanted to tell her that she needn't have bothered. Anything she wore in this house was never going to stay on her for long.

"Hey," he said, getting up to kiss her lips. "Sleep well?"

"Like a dream. Where is everyone?"

"Adam's running errands, and Troy's in the gym."

"The gym?"

"We have one in the basement behind the garage." He patted his naked torso, giving her a graphic reminder of the impressive six-packs they all sported. "How do you think we maintain our beautiful bodies?"

Porcha laughed. "The same way you keep your modesty in check, I imagine."

"What, we have something to be modest about?" He gaped at her. "You sure know how to wound."

"Someone has to keep your collective egos in check."

"Yeah, babe," he said, pinching her cheek. "But that someone sure as hell ain't you."

"Really?" She flashed what he guessed was supposed to be a deliberately flirtatious glance. "Then what am I doing here?"

He growled at her and bit her neck. "Like you don't already know the answer to that one. Want some breakfast?"

"Just fruit and coffee will be fine." She headed for the kitchen. "I'll help myself."

"What happens now?" she asked, wandering back into the living room, a half-drunk mug of coffee in her hand.

"About your situation?" Beck shrugged. "Let's wait until the boss joins us. I dare say he has a cunning plan already figured out."

"How do you spend your time between assignments?" she asked. "I gather Adam enjoys his kitchen and Troy has his computers. What about you?"

"Oh, I'm into wheels. Unlike Adam, I didn't come from a privileged background. I was stealing cars before I was old enough to see over the steering wheels and drive them away because that's what *big* men did." He shrugged. "I guess I've always been a speed junkie."

"Didn't that land you in trouble with the law? 'Grand theft auto' they call it on this side of the pond, don't they?"

"Yes, they do, and yes, it could have. Fortunately, I joined the army before it got out of control, got into a brawl with Troy over something stupid, and that's why you see me here today."

"You and Troy hit it off straightaway?"

"We *hit* each other straightaway," Beck said, laughing at the memory. "Over a woman, I think it was."

Porcha rolled her eyes. "Figures."

"The next day he sought me out to apologise. Not that he had anything to apologise for." He flashed her a grin. "Boys will be boys. Anyway, we got chatting, found we got along, and have been buddies ever since."

"I see." Porcha put her cup down, wandered over to the window, and stared out at the sparkling water. "Another lovely day," she remarked.

Beck didn't answer. His gaze was focused on her ass confined in those tight shorts, and he was too busy admiring what he saw to bother with words. He'd spent one hell of a night not sleeping a lot, too wound up by thoughts of their sexy little sub to get any rest. He and the guys had a kind of unspoken agreement not to masturbate anywhere other than the playroom, which meant they never did it in private. It was the sort of control issue that Troy was tough on. His discipline, his ability to wait longer than most people could stand in dangerous situations, had kept them all alive on more than one occasion. It was fun to run that sort of control into their sex games.

Or had been until this little minx happened into their well-ordered lives and turned them on their asses.

He walked behind her and wrapped his arms round her tits. Adam went for legs, but Beck was a breast man. Troy…well Troy liked variety and went for the whole package. Beck's hands sank into the ample flesh, kneading and caressing until she leaned back against him and softly moaned. Her sweet ass agitated his erection, and this time, alone with their tempting little sub, he had no intention of holding back.

"Take your shorts off," he said gruffly, "and submit to me."

Without hesitation she turned to face him, unzipped, and let her shorts fall to the floor. He ran his gaze lazily down the length of her body. She was wearing another of her tiny thongs but didn't remove it because he hadn't told her to. That was okay. Beck would fuck her with it on. Her bra, too. He'd pull those big tits out of the cups and torment her nipples while he fucked that sassy ass.

"Do you wanna be fucked, sugar?"

"Yes, master." She licked her lips and then lowered her eyes. "Very much."

"Take your top off."

When she did so, he wasn't surprised that her bra matched the thong. She hadn't brought much stuff with her in the bag she hastily packed, so a lot of it had to have been underwear. Not that it mattered much. One of Adam's errands was to pick her up a load more, but of their choosing this time.

"Pull your tits out the top," he said. "I wanna see those big nipples get hard for me."

She did as he asked, expectancy and excitement radiating from her expression.

"Come here."

He sat down and pulled her across his knee. "You wanna be spanked?"

"I want to do whatever it takes to please you."

Beck chuckled. "I know you do, babe." He brought a hand down fairly hard on her backside, at the same time reaching beneath her, pushing the front of her sodden thong aside and finding her clit. "Can you feel my prick pushing into your gut?" When she nodded, he carried on tormenting her with his hands and his voice. "It's that big 'cause you make me crazy. I wanna fuck you so much that I'm in physical pain. Will you let me fuck you senseless, sweet Porcha?"

"Yes, sir." She panted the words. "I need you to do that, if it'll please you."

"I can't decide whether to fuck your ass, your cunt, or your mouth." He tilted his head and ran his gaze along the length of her body, trying to decide. "Which would you prefer?"

"All three."

Beck roared with laughter. "I'll see what I can do." He spanked her again, harder this time. "Adam's getting some surprises for you."

"What are they?"

"Well, if I told you that, they wouldn't be a surprise, would they now?"

"No, master."

"Kneel on the floor."

She did so, and Beck shed his shorts. He wasn't wearing anything else, and his erection sprang free—proud, angry, and pulsating like crazy—as soon as he lowered his zipper.

"Suck me off, babe."

She slid to the floor and attached her lips to his cock, her hand joining the party as she skilfully massaged his testicles and sucked him deeper into her mouth. *Fuck it, Troy's right to say she's good at this!* He didn't want to think about the bastard who'd taught her or how he'd made her do it in front of his guests just to humiliate her. All he could think about was the cataclysmic climax building deep inside his core.

Adam didn't have much to say about the women they played with as a rule, but he'd droned on endlessly about how special Porcha was, right from the moment they first met. That he'd taken matters into his own hands yesterday, instigated matters in the playroom, and spoken so highly of her afterward sealed the deal. Troy had expressed similar opinions after fucking her in Tampa, indicating that they were, as usual, singing from the same song sheet. What would come of their joint obsession, Beck had no idea. The farther she sucked him into her mouth, playfully running her tongue repeatedly over his slit, the harder it was to think about anything else, so he gave up trying.

Beck placed his hands behind Porcha's head and pushed himself deeper into her mouth.

"That's it, Porcha. Make me come for you." He ground himself into the back of her throat. "You're killing me. I'm gonna shoot it any second." He knocked her hands away from his balls and grabbed the base of his cock. "Shit, here it comes!"

He fountained an endless stream of semen into her mouth. She drank it down, licking her lips to ensure she hadn't missed any. All the time her eyes never left his face, as though seeking his approval.

Beck collapsed, panting, into a chair and pulled her onto his lap. He captured her lips in a deep, drugging kiss, tasting himself as his tongue foraged her mouth with a hunger that seemed to grow sharper the more he got to know her. Her lips softened beneath his as she leaned her glorious tits against him and kissed him back with interest.

Beck broke the kiss, already hard again.

"Your ass this time," he said. "Get on the floor."

As soon as she was in position on a rug, he moved behind her, wondering if he ought to get some lube. One finger in her anus was enough to tell him it would be unnecessary.

"You're desperate, aren't you?" he said, kissing her cute butt as he worked another finger into her, making absolutely sure she was ready for him. "You're the greediest little sub we've ever had."

"I need you to fuck me," she said, her voice a strangled moan. "Punish me afterward for asking, but I need you right now."

She pushed her ass at him to emphasise her point, and Beck was lost. He shouldn't allow her to call the shots and ought to punish her by holding back. Tie her hands behind her and make her stand in the corner with lowered head. Bring her to the brink of orgasm and then leave her dangling. Something, anything. Troy would insist if he was here.

But Troy wasn't here. He wasn't the one with a cock that burned for action not five minutes after being sucked off. Beck was damned if he could hold back now. What Troy didn't know wouldn't hurt him.

Beck eased an inch of his cock into her anus.

"You all right with that?" he asked. "Need any lube?"

"No, I'm soaking wet already."

Beck chuckled. "Yeah, remind me to punish you for that."

He eased into her, a task made simple because she kept shoving back to help him. Beck was proud of his dimensions, but Porcha had no trouble at all accommodating him.

"You love my cock up your ass, don't you, sugar?"

"Yes." She expelled several short, desperate breaths. "Do I have it all?"

He slammed into her, his balls smashing hard against her ass. "You do now." Beck groaned. "Like that, do you?"

"Yes, master. It's wonderful."

Beck reached for her breasts, still hanging from the top of her bra. He pinched the rock-hard nipples until she moaned and then mashed one entire breast between both hands, hard. At the same time he increased the pace of his thrusts into her ass. Porcha screamed as a climax claimed her.

"Fuck me, Beck. Go deeper. I need to feel you all."

"Christ!"

"Beck, it's still not enough. I can't feel you. Just fuck me!"

He smashed into her, sweating with the speed of his movements as she rode her climax and instigated his own. He came in a gush, sensing a second orgasm sweeping though Porcha as she moved with him, their explosive amalgamation sucking them both completely dry.

They collapsed in a heap on the rug as a single round of applause rang out. They glanced up and saw Troy standing there, slick from his workout, completely naked, and very aroused.

"That was quite a performance," he said.

"Glad you approve." Beck grinned as he moved Porcha's head from his chest and stood up.

"Troy!" Porcha climbed to her feet as well and kissed his lips. "Do you always work out naked?"

"Always."

"Isn't it dangerous?"

"Only if you don't know what you're doing. Talking of which, there's something you could do for me that won't require any instruction. Wrap your legs round my waist, babe. I've got something here that you might enjoy."

Arms entwined round his neck, she leapt athletically from the floor and captured his waist with her long legs. Troy supported her beneath her ass and guided her onto his erection. He didn't lean against a wall to help support her weight, but Beck would have accused him of being a wuss if he had. If they weren't fit enough to support a little thing like Porcha, who couldn't weigh more than one twenty max, and fuck her at the same time, then it was time for them to retire.

"Take it all, babe," he said, driving into her. "I've been anticipating this all the time I've been pumping that damned iron."

Her exposed nipples rubbed against the hairs on his chest as they moved, driving them both on.

"You like being fucked off the floor?"

"Yes, master. It's a real out-of-body experience."

Beck and Troy exchanged a glance. "Well, if you like it so much, I think we have a few gadgets that might make it even better."

"Troy, I—"

"I know, I can feel you closing in on me." He grinned over her shoulder at Beck. "Well, if Beck let you break the rules—"

"How long were you watching?" Beck demanded to know.

"Long enough." Troy thrust into her a little harder. "Push down on it, darlin'. Don't worry, I won't drop you. Yeah, that's it." Troy expelled a long, anguished sigh. "Fuck it, Porcha, you know how to drive a guy crazy."

"Take that as a compliment, babe," Beck advised. "Not many women can make Troy lose his famous control."

"This one sure as fuck can."

Beck could see her limbs trembling. "She's about to come, Troy."

"Ride it, babe. Go on, it's all for you. I'm fucking you hard. You like it hard, don't you? The harder the better, and I'm rock hard right now." Troy moved his entire pelvis with his next thrust. "Feel that, do you? Take it all, honey. This one's for you."

"Troy!"

She bit into his shoulder, drawing blood as she jerked and then spasmed on his rigid shaft. Beck noticed her entire body shake as she threw her head back and screamed. Troy bit down on her nipple, presumably in retaliation for her drawing blood, and groaned as he emptied himself into her.

Troy took his time lowering Porcha into a chair and flopping down next to her. Beck sat on her other side.

"Well," Troy said. "That ain't a bad way to start the day. Beats the hell out of pumping iron, anyway."

They all laughed.

"After a night's reflection, are you still happy with this arrangement?" Troy asked Porcha. "You haven't had more than one man at a time before. Sure you can take it?"

"If you even think about calling a halt I swear I'll find a way to bring swift and brutal punishments cascading on your head...and other places."

"Just checking," Troy said easily. "Because from now on in, there's no going softly. You *will* do as we ask, whenever we ask it. No more relaxing the rules because you're a rookie."

Porcha lowered her eyes, presumably because she understood he meant it. "No, sir."

"Okay, babe, just needed to be sure that you're good with this."

"Thank goodness that she is." Beck stood up. "I need a shower."

"Me, too," Porcha said, but she looked toward Troy for permission before she moved.

"Off you go. Shower alone, Beck," he said. "I'll get clean, too, and we'll meet down here in ten. We need to discuss strategy as soon as Adam gets back, and if we keep fucking her we'll never get anywhere."

Chapter Eight

"We'll take good care of her."

"You damn well better. She means a lot to me."

"Yeah," Troy said down the secure phone line. "She told us. What have you heard about the death of her husband? Has it been confirmed?"

"You have doubts?" Georgio's voice resonated with surprise. "She sent me the picture she received. Looks real enough to me."

"It does, but there's been no report of his death, that's what bothers me. If rivals took him out, you know as well as I do that they'd shout about it, long and loud because they'd wanna take over his territory."

"He never leaves her for long," Georgio said. "He'd been gone for two weeks before she got that picture, which is the maximum amount of time for him. It's now a month. If he was still alive, he'd have got word to her."

"If he's at liberty to talk to anyone."

"If he has been taken, why would anyone want to pretend that he's dead? Everyone knows that the sick fuck played cruel games with her, but he never let her in on his business secrets. If they *are* looking for something, she'd be the last one to know where it was."

"That's what bothers me." Troy was aware of Porcha and then Beck entering the study as he spoke. "How did all those men Porcha saw swarming over her home get in there if it was so well guarded? And why wasn't there a report of it on the news media? The police know nothing about it, either. I've checked."

"I see what you mean."

"Is that Georgio?" Porcha asked. "Can I talk to him?"

Troy pulled her into his lap and switched to speakerphone. "Someone here is anxious to talk to you."

"Georgio, how are you?"

"More to the point, how are you, sweetheart? Are those Neanderthals taking good care of you?"

"Hey, who are you calling a Neanderthal?" Beck demanded.

"They are doing things for me that you can't begin to imagine," Porcha said happily.

"Unfortunately, I think I can." There was a smile in Georgio's voice, full of Italian-American charm. "Still, better them than that brute of a husband of yours, I guess."

"Thanks for sending them, Georgio. I was mad at you, but I realize now that you were right. I *did* need help, and I feel safe for the first time in two weeks."

"That was kind of the idea, babe. You still there, Troy?"

"Yes, sir."

"I take it you're gonna try and discover who's out to get our little girl?"

"Believe it."

"Then what do you need from me?"

"Right now, nothing. Just stay alert, Georgio."

"Why?" Porcha asked, alarm in her voice. "No one knows about my friendship with Georgio. Well, no one who'd wish either of us any harm."

Troy quirked a brow. "I'll get back to you when we've decided what action we're going to take."

"I await your call." Georgio blew a kiss down the line. "That was for Porcha, by the way, not for any of you ugly lot."

"Glad to hear it."

Adam had joined them midway through the call, and all three men laughed as Troy disconnected, giving Georgio the finger even though he wasn't there to appreciate the gesture.

Troy tipped Porcha off his lap and led them all back into the living room.

"Right," he said when they'd all taken seats. "In case you didn't hear what I said to Georgio, here's a summary of what I think. Sal Gonzalez may or may not be dead. If he is, why hasn't the news leaked?"

"Good point," Adam said.

"Yeah, and here's another one. He's always well protected. How did someone get to him without a gun battle between him and his bodyguards?"

"Unless one or all of the bodyguards were in on it," Beck suggested.

"Precisely." Troy turned toward Porcha. "Who would he have had with him?"

"Woollard went everywhere with him. Apart from that, I wouldn't know." Porcha shrugged. "He employed twenty men in different capacities. I never knew where they were and what they were doing. He would have taken at least one other with him to Mexico and had some of the men he employs down there meet him when he arrived."

"So the hit could have been arranged from either end," Adam said.

"It could," Troy agreed, "but I think it was this end because of the way they got into the Jupiter house without the alarm being raised. It was too well orchestrated for it to have been coordinated from Mexico."

Adam and Beck both nodded.

"Good point," Beck said, "but I still don't understand what the hell they were doing."

"Nor me, but I think the perpetrator was looking for something specific."

"Well, we're never gonna know what that was because Porcha didn't get back into the house," Adam said.

"Not yet she didn't." Troy flashed a smug grin and waited for the others to catch up. Adam got there first.

"You wanna break in and see what's missing?"

"Break in?" Troy dredged up an innocent expression. "That would be against the law."

Beck laughed. "I dare say the lady of the house has a key, and the code to the alarm, always assuming it's been reset."

All eyes turned toward Porcha.

"I'm up for a sentimental return to my roots," she said.

"Not you, babe." Troy spoke with authority. "We'll go tonight, but you stay put here."

"Fine, and how, precisely, will you know what's missing?"

Adam's grin was full of admiration. "She has a point there."

"And she can look after herself," Beck added.

Adam nodded. "True, and I'd feel better if she was with us, where we can keep an eye on her."

"We're getting ahead of ourselves here," Troy said, holding up his hands. "We don't know who broke into the house, if they're still there, and for that matter, if we'd be walking into a bullet fest."

"You're right," Adam agreed. "Hell if I'll risk letting Porcha into the middle of that."

"If the bad guys, and I use the term advisedly, are gone," Troy said to Porcha, "who would be at the house now?"

"The guards, and they live in a bungalow in the grounds."

"Assuming they're still alive," Beck said.

"If they'd been killed that *would* have hit the media."

"Yeah, but they could have been chased off," Troy reasoned. "They failed in their duty, and assuming they don't know their boss is dead…If he is, then they'd probably prefer to disappear rather than face his wrath. I get the impression that he doesn't take kindly to failure in the ranks."

"He *is* dead," Porcha said, hugging herself. "I'd know if he wasn't. Don't ask me how," she added when all three men looked at her. "He just had this way of getting into my head, no matter where he was. I realize now that that feeling left me on the day we ran into all that trouble at the house."

Troy wasn't convinced but let it pass.

"Do the guards have access to the house?" he asked instead.

"No."

"Forget finding out what's missing," Troy said. "We just need to know if the house is secure."

"Well," Porcha said, idly running her index finger along her lower lip as she pondered the problem. "If it's all shut up tight, the alarm will be set. I could call the company, say I got a missed call about the alarm going off and see what they say."

Troy reached for the nearest phone. "Do it."

"I'll need to switch my phone on. The security company's number's programmed into it."

"Okay, but turn it right off again."

Porcha fired up her phone, waited to get a signal, and found the number she needed. She punched the digits into the phone Troy handed to her and switched her cell off again. She got through, gave her password, said her spiel, and listened.

"Okay, the message must have been older than I realized. Thanks for putting my mind at rest. I've been abroad for a while and out of cell-phone range. No, no, everything's fine. Thanks for your help."

"Well?" Troy asked when Porcha hung up.

"The alarm went off two weeks ago, almost to the day." She glanced at the piece of paper, upon which she'd jotted down notes. "The dates coincide with my returning to the house and seeing all hell breaking loose."

"But the police didn't attend?"

"No, the instructions Sal gave the alarm company were to report to him or Woollard if it went off but not to call the police. They say they phoned both numbers. Sal wouldn't want to give the police an excuse to enter his property. Besides, he never seriously thought anyone would have the balls to break in, and if they did, he'd get his own people to deal with it."

"But the alarm's set again now?"

"Yes, which means there's no one in the property. Or, there could be but no one's home right now."

"So, why would someone break in and then set the alarm again?" Troy asked.

"Because it was an inside job," Adam and Beck said together.

"I could call the security guards in their bungalow and ask them what's happening?" Porcha suggested.

"Probably not a good…No, actually, give me the number of the hut," Troy said.

Once again, Porcha turned her phone on, jotted down the number, and scribbled it down for Troy. He got up, went back into the study, and called the number from the secure line. No one would be able to trace the call back to them. The phone was answered on the second ring.

"Who's Philby?" Troy asked, heading back to the living room.

"Head of Sal's security detail."

"Well," Troy said, sitting down, stretching his legs in front of him and crossing them at the ankles. "If someone's killed his boss, he knows nothing about it. He's manning the phone like nothing in the world is wrong."

"What the hell's going on, Troy?" Adam asked.

Troy leaned an elbow on the arm of his chair and dropped his chin into his cupped hand. "I don't have a definite answer. What I *think* is that Sal Gonzalez is dead and that he was ambushed by someone within his own ranks. What I don't understand is why all those people were swarming over his property in broad daylight. Did you actually see them, babe?"

"I saw figures dashing about the grounds, but Kevin turned the car round before we got close enough for me to see faces."

"So, for all you know, they could have been your own guys, staging the break-in for your benefit."

Porcha shrugged. "I guess. But why?"

"To frighten you off," Troy said slowly. "Because someone, whoever staged this fiasco, was interested in you."

"Me!" Porcha jumped to her feet. "But why?"

Troy reached out, touched her arm, and she slowly subsided back into her seat.

"In that case, why not just hide in the house and let her walk in?"

"Because whoever did this was playing a double game. He or they invited the guards to ransack the house, take whatever they wanted, knowing that Porcha was due home at any moment and she'd see it all."

"Presumably, they'd also know that her driver would get her out of there fast." Adam frowned. "Unless he was in on it, too?"

"I could call them both," Porcha said. "Didn't you say that might be a way to go?"

"No, I don't think they were involved. Very few people know about this, and it explains the demand for fictitious diamonds and the arrival of those thugs at the hotel you were in, babe. They probably put a tracking device on your car so they knew where you were holed up, but you thought Kevin had betrayed you and bolted." He paused. "Straight to the only place you thought was safe."

"The apartment?"

"The perpetrator wanted to take over Sal's business and his wife." Troy focused his gaze on Porcha's troubled face. "And it was someone who knew all his secrets, or had access to them, including the apartment. Any idea who wanted you badly enough to do all that, Porcha?"

"Woollard," she said, the air leaving her lungs in an audible whoosh. "It could only be that sick bastard Woollard. Sal might not have told him about the apartment, but he was in a position to find out, what with the two of them being so tight."

Chapter Nine

Porcha shook her head. "I don't believe it," she said softly, standing to pace the room, too agitated to remain in one place. "There are many things about him that repel me, but I would have sworn he was completely loyal to Sal."

"Don't let it get to you, babe." Troy stood up, cut her off midpace, took her hand, and pulled her onto his lap as he resumed his seat. "Honour amongst thieves isn't all it's cracked up to be."

She leaned against his chest and sighed. "Easy for you to say."

"He doesn't know you're onto him, and that gives us an edge."

"Troy's right," Beck said. "He usually is, and it's fucking annoying."

Adam laughed. "Too right. Anyway, I reckon Woollard deliberately staged that fiasco at your house just when he knew you'd be on your way back."

"How did he know that? I could have been another hour or more."

"Simple." Troy shrugged. "If he did put a tracking device on the car, he'd have known where you were every step of the way. It's what I'd have done in his place."

"If it *was* on the car," Adam said.

"Oh fuck!" Troy and Beck said together.

"See." Adam winked at Porcha. "He doesn't always think of everything."

Porcha frowned. "What has he overlooked?"

"They could have put something on you." Troy looked annoyed not to have thought of it sooner. "Well, not actually on your person but on something you carry with you all the time."

"In which case they'll know where I am now."

"Exactly." Adam grimaced. "Can I borrow your purse?"

"Sure."

Adam tipped the contents on the table and went through them one by one, discarding anything unsuitable for hiding a bug in. Then he turned the large purse inside out, feeling along the seams for anything that didn't sit right. Beck produced a weird-looking device from the study that looked a bit like a wand. Adam ran it all over the bag and shook his head.

"It's clean."

He repeated the process with the larger items from her purse, her cell phone and iPad, again with negative results.

"Then it has to have been a tracking device, unless Kevin was in on it, and it has to be Woollard," Troy said doggedly. "He wanted to scare you shitless, which he pretty well managed to do, and then ride to the rescue." Troy squeezed her hand. "You said yourself that you didn't return his interest in you but that you *did* trust him. He would have known that."

"So you think he did all this, killed my husband and presumably took over his business, just because he wanted me?" Porcha shook her head. "It seems a bit extreme, even for a megalomaniac like Woollard."

"The three of us would do a damned sight more than that if it meant we could keep you to ourselves forever," Beck told her, for once not smiling.

"Damned right," Adam agreed.

"We'd die to keep you alive," Troy said simply.

Beck nodded. "No question about it."

"Thanks," Porcha said, moved by their obvious sincerity, especially since she had only known them for a couple of days. "Let's hope that doesn't become necessary."

"It goes with the territory in our line of work," Adam said almost casually.

"If it is Woollard, why all the theatrics?" Porcha asked. "I know I had my cell switched off, but he has my e-mail address. It would have been a lot easier just to send me a damned message, surely?"

Troy shook his head and smiled grimly. "Like I said, he wanted you to sweat a bit first. He wanted you to be really frightened so that you'd trust him. Better the devil you know and all that." Troy shifted his position, and Porcha instinctively leaned a little more of her weight against his broad chest, taking comfort from his strength and the resolution in his expression. "I'm willing to bet he was about to make a move on you at the apartment, which was why he had someone watching to make sure the coast was clear. Only problem is, we turned up and spoiled the party for him."

"How inconsiderate can you get?" Beck asked.

"Unless he knows who we are, he has no idea where you are now," Adam said. "He didn't expect you to get away, so he's all out of options. My guess is that he will have to e-mail you before much longer."

Porcha slid off Troy's knee, fired up her iPad, and checked her e-mail.

"Nothing yet."

"Good, then we have time to think of an alternative strategy."

"Does Woollard know of your friendship with Georgio?" Beck asked.

Porcha lifted her shoulders. "I didn't tell him, and I can't think of any reason why Sal would have."

"Sal didn't tell him about the apartment, but it looks like Woollard knew," Troy pointed out.

"Just as a matter of interest, how come Sal let you stay in touch with Georgio if he was so protective?" Adam asked.

She shrugged. "I'm not really sure. He knew of our history and didn't see him as a threat, I guess."

Beck frowned. "Do you think Georgio's in danger?"

"Unless Woollard's into hacking e-mail accounts—"

"I wouldn't put anything past him," Porcha said, shuddering.

"Georgio sends all his stuff through remote servers. They can't be traced back to him, and he didn't sign any of the stuff he sent to you, did he, babe?" Troy asked.

"No, but if he's got into my account he wouldn't need to be Einstein to figure out who I'd contacted and why." Porcha dropped her face against Troy's shoulder. "Shit, this is getting messy!"

"So, three guys turning up on your doorstep could only mean Georgio sent them," Troy said, gently massaging the back of her head. "Woollard would know what he does."

Porcha covered her mouth with one hand. "Does that mean that I've placed Georgio in danger?"

"Don't worry about that. Georgio can look after himself." Troy ran his large hands down her back in a manner that reassured. "But he does need to be warned about Woollard."

Troy lifted Porcha from his lap and went into the study to make the call. He returned after a few minutes, grim faced.

"He now knows the score."

But Porcha could see that Troy was worried, which only increased her own fear.

"What now, boss?" Adam asked.

"I guess we wait for Woollard to get in touch." Troy shrugged. "We don't know where he is, so we can't go after him."

"True, but I hate waiting."

"I'm sure we can think of something to do to pass the time and take our minds off things," Beck said, grinning at Porcha.

"Any other suggestions?" Troy asked.

"I think Woollard's camped out in the Jupiter house," Adam said, "and that we ought to pay him a little visit."

"Because if he wants to take over from Sal, he has to move in on his property, too, otherwise Sal's foot soldiers might not follow him." Troy nodded in agreement. "Very likely, but it's a long journey across state, and I don't want to make it unless we're sure he's there.

Besides, he knows we're with Porcha and might be expecting us. I'm not saying we couldn't get past his security—"

"Glad to hear it," Beck said. "For a moment there, I thought you were going soft on me."

"Oh, we'd get in all right, especially with a little insider knowledge to give us the edge." Troy tweaked Porcha's nose. "But I don't think it's an acceptable risk right now. There has to be another way."

"We could be proactive, get Porcha to ring Woollard and set things in motion," Adam mused. "That way there's less chance of Georgio being targeted."

Troy rubbed his chin. "Or, assuming Woollard had access to Porcha's e-mail, we could get her to send a message to Georgio, saying that she feels safer now and doesn't need us anymore. Especially since we appear to be more interested in getting into her pants than in keeping her safe—"

"Good thinking," Adam said. "That'll make him furious."

Beck nodded. "And furious men make mistakes when they're thinking with their dicks."

"Right." Troy grimaced. "She could tell Georgio that she's going…going where?"

"That I'm going home to England," Porcha said. "That I've arranged to meet a guy who can get me a passport. I could say I'm convinced that once I get back to England no one will follow me there and I'll be safe."

"Might work," Adam mused. "Obviously we'll be there, not you, ready to take Woollard down."

"I'd like to go, too."

"Absolutely not!" three male voices said in unison.

"Sorry, babe," Troy added, "but we don't know how many people he'll have with him. We'll have our hands full and won't be able to protect you."

"I don't need protecting."

"The hell you don't!" Porcha was still on Troy's knee. Beck crouched in front of her and ran his index finger down the length of her leg. "Leave this to us, Porcha. It's what we do, and we do it well."

"He's right," Adam said. "We're not trying to dominate you, if that's what you're thinking. We promised that would only happen when we play our sex games, and we'll keep our word."

"But this is different." Troy smiled at her. "We've only just found you, and we have no intention of getting you killed."

"Oh, you three!" Porcha sprang from Troy's lap and threw her hands in the air. "What do I have to do to convince you that I can take care of myself?"

Beck stood beside her, grinning, obviously about to make one of his off-the-wall comments. It was too good an opportunity to pass up. Porcha walked up to him and with a soft sigh leaned her back against his chest.

"You're right," she said. "All of you."

"We are?"

She sensed Beck's confusion and played the helpless female for all her worth. Catching sight of Troy's lazy half smile in the periphery of her vision, she sensed he knew what she was about to do, but he didn't warn her off.

"Rub my shoulders, Beck," she said, wiggling her ass against him. "I'm so tense I feel I could break in half."

Beck grinned. "My pleasure, babe."

The moment he applied his hands to her shoulders she sprang into action. Grabbing one of his arms over her shoulder, she caught him off balance and used his body weight against him, applied a swift kick to the back of his knees, and sent him flat on his ass.

Adam and Troy roared with laughter.

"Just proving a point," Porcha said sweetly.

Beck sprang to his feet, pulled her into his arms, and growled at her. "You're still not coming with us!"

"No, you're not," Troy agreed. "You took Beck by surprise, but Woollard knows what you're capable of and won't underestimate you."

"But feel free to do that to Beck again any time," Adam said, still laughing. "I'd pay to see a repeat performance."

"I'm sorry I put you on your ass, Beck," she said meekly.

"Oh, think nothing of it." He grabbed her round the waist and swung her in the air. "It's nothing compared to what I have planned for your sweet rear later on. Forget about all that bollocks about revenge being a dish best served cold. Steaming hot's the only way to get even, in my view."

She fluttered her lashes at him. "Is that a promise?"

"As to your coming with us, Porcha," Troy said. "I still haven't decided if we ought to even send that e-mail, so it could be a moot point. I'm gonna think on it for the rest of the day." He frowned. "Part of me thinks we're missing something here, and I hate going into anything half cocked."

"That's not a problem I've noticed you wrestling with," she said, grinning.

The other two guys merely grunted, clearly used to Troy taking time over important decisions.

"I guess I'd better get in the gym for an hour," Beck complained, putting Porcha back on her feet.

Adam glanced between Troy and Beck. "You two look pretty damned smug. Did I miss some fun when I was out earlier?"

Beck shrugged. "Porcha helped us to feel more comfortable, is all."

"Come here, Porcha."

She responded to Adam's commanding tone on autopilot, moving to stand in front of him with lowered eyes. Beck shrugged and made for the garage. Troy headed for the study.

"Don't wear her out," he said as he left. "We're gonna have a big party tonight, and Porcha's the star attraction."

"Gotcha!"

Porcha lifted her eyes sufficiently to see Adam make himself more comfortable on the couch. He leaned back, ran one arm along its back, and splayed his legs, giving her a good view of the bulge in his pants.

"Take your clothes off," he said. "Why are you wearing any indoors anyway?"

"Troy said I had to get dressed after he fucked me, master. He said when we have business to discuss it's too distracting if I'm naked."

Adam chuckled. "Damn right it is!"

Porcha was wearing a short denim skirt. She unzipped it and let it fall slowly to the floor. She lifted her top over her head and threw that aside, too. Then she stood where she was, hands neatly folded, awaiting his next order.

"And the rest."

He rubbed his erection through his pants as he watched her remove her bra and thong.

"Stand with your legs apart so I can see your pussy, and then play with your tits. Make me hot for you, baby."

Porcha did as he asked, moulding her large breasts through her hands, allowing the hard nipples to peak over the top, her eyes never leaving his face. Adam inhaled sharply when she ran her tongue along her lower lip and pulled it through her teeth. Even so, he appeared in no hurry to touch her and made her stand there for a long time touching first her tits and then her cunt, sliding her fingers in and out, agitating her clit as her juices poured. She was close to orgasm, just because she was touching herself and Adam was watching her with such fascination—to say nothing of his raging hard-on—but she knew better than to come without his permission.

As she continued to put on a show for him, Porcha became more and more desperate for Adam's cock. She rotated her head, her hair cascading over her face, lips parting in desperation. Finally, just when she thought she couldn't take any more waiting, she heard Adam's zipper being yanked down. She glanced up just as a huge, very angry erection sprang free from his pants. He threw his tank top off, displaying a six-pack to match Troy's and Beck's, and beckoned to her with one finger.

"Come and kneel here." He tapped the floor between his legs. "Submit to me, Porcha. Do it now."

Porcha didn't hesitate. As soon as she was in position, he started giving her orders in such an authoritative way that excitement ricocheted through her. She absolutely loved commanding men, and it appeared that she'd pitched up in a house with three of them, all anxious to fuck her. When did she get to be so lucky?

Adam ordered her to rub his cock between her breasts. He moaned as she did so but made no move to touch her. Even when he ordered her to suck him and she felt his prick swell to even greater proportions inside her mouth, he kept his hands to himself. She turned round and knelt with her ass in the air so he could rub his erection down the split in her ass. It felt like heaven, even though Adam continued to sit with his hands laced behind his head and didn't lay a finger on her.

He had her turning cartwheels for half an hour, still without touching her. Who would have thought that being admired but not touched would be one of the most erotic experiences of her life? To see such lust in his eye, to watch his cock growing to impossible proportions, to be aware how much he wanted her and yet still had the discipline not to touch. She desperately wanted to be spanked, or punished in some other way, just to heighten her already frantic anticipation. She realized now that by not touching her, that was precisely what he was doing.

Eventually, just when she thought she couldn't take the waiting for a moment longer, he ordered her to straddle him. But it was obvious that he still didn't plan to use his hands. She was expected to do all the work, and that was just fine with her. She sank down onto that glorious cock, sighing as it invaded her cunt like a laser, sending sensation sweeping through every inch of her body as she greedily took him all. He didn't move a muscle but simply watched her as she closed her vagina tightly round him, her cunt on fire with the deep-seated need she felt.

"Do you need to come, little one?" he asked.

"Yes, master, if it would please you."

"How much do you need it? What would you be prepared to do in return for permission to orgasm, sweet Porcha?"

"Chain me down and whip me, sir." Porcha's voice was an anguished moan as she rode Adam's cock without any help from him. He continued to sit stock-still, his control extraordinary. "You're so big, master. I need to feel you hard inside me."

"Feel it, babe."

Suddenly, Adam was all action. He thrust into her so hard and deep that she cried out with a combination of pleasure and pain, meeting him halfway as he picked up the pace, absolutely loving the feel of his huge prick invading her body.

"You're so fucking tight, Porcha, you're driving me insane. Come on, babe, let's do it. Ride it, sweetheart, take what you want. You can come."

Music to her ears. Porcha thrashed down on his cock, pushing one heavy breast so close to his mouth that he instinctively caught the nipple between his teeth and bit it. The sensation was almost too much, and she screamed as she climaxed, throwing her head back and glorying in the endless waves of pleasure that spread through her like a starburst.

Adam was still rock hard inside her when she eventually stopped coming. *How does he do that?* She lowered her eyes and moved more slowly.

"Thank you, master," she said softly.

"Get on the floor. I want your ass."

He took it, hard and fast, making her come again moments before he did. He collapsed on top of her, breathless and sweating, when he was finally spent.

"Remind me to punish you later," he said, laughing as he rolled to one side and pulled her, naked, on top of him.

Chapter Ten

"Is it safe to come in now?" Troy asked, poking his head round the door.

Adam pulled himself up on one elbow and grinned. "Since when do you bother to ask?"

Troy had listened to Adam and Porcha making out. From the sounds of things, Adam was in one of his *keeping his hands to himself* moods, for which he was famous. Even Troy had trouble maintaining that much control, but Adam had never told him and Beck how he managed it. Troy would give a lot to know where he went to inside his head to resist the almost-overwhelming temptation that Porcha must have presented him with. What man with a pulse could resist getting their hands on those glorious tits? Still, Troy didn't blame Adam for keeping his mouth shut about his technique. They might be buddies, workmates, and housemates, together practically 24/7, but they were still individuals with secrets of their own that they didn't share.

Troy strolled into the room and smiled at the tangle of sweaty limbs on the rug. Porcha looked up when she heard him but immediately lowered her eyes again.

"Go and get showered, both of you," he said. "I'll see to lunch."

Adam stood and helped Porcha to her feet. "That was quite something, babe," he said, pulling her into one of the slow, incendiary kisses that he favored.

"I aim to oblige," she said when he released her, skipping toward the stairs.

"Don't bother to put any clothes on when you're clean," Troy said to her. "We prefer you the way you are now."

She flashed the type of naughty grin that would earn her a good hiding later.

"Your wish is my command, boss man," she said.

Troy rolled his eyes at Adam. "Damned right it is."

"What do you have planned for tonight?" Adam asked.

"Does it have something to do with this?" Beck asked, bounding up the stairs from the garage and handing a package to Troy. "I just went out for a run and caught the delivery man on my way back."

"Ah yes, that would be it."

Smiling, Troy showed his buddies what he'd purchased and told them what he had planned for the evening.

"Christ!" Beck scrubbed a hand down his face. "Do you think she can take it?"

"I think she'll take everything we ask her to and still come back for more."

"Roll on this evening," Adam said with feeling. "I've just fucked her, and I'm rock hard again already." He shook his head. "What is it about her?"

"Hell if I know," Troy said, "but I feel it, too."

"And me," Beck agreed, nodding. "Best not to fight it. Just go with the flow and see where it leads."

"I think we know where that will be." Adam raised his eyes to the upper floors.

"No," Troy said quietly. "Well, yes, actually, but there's a damned sight more to it than that. She's gotten right to me."

"No arguments there," the other two said, practically at once.

Adam and Beck both headed for the shower while Troy pulled together a sandwich lunch. He thought about Porcha as he worked, about the profound impact she'd had on their lives in the short time they'd known her, and where they'd stand with her once they'd sorted her problems. The thought of her returning to England wrenched at his gut. If he had any say in the matter, it wasn't gonna happen, and he was pretty sure that the others felt exactly the same way. They'd never factored a permanent woman into their thinking, but Porcha was special. Her sort came along once in a lifetime—if you were lucky— and they'd be idiots if they let her go.

Troy and his buddies had shared so many women in the past that he'd lost count. He'd certainly forgotten most of their names. None of them had left even a temporary impression. Porcha, on the other hand, had breezed into their lives and turned their organized existence firmly on its ass without being aware that she'd done it.

Against all the odds, it appeared that the unthinkable had happened. In just a few short days, Troy Anderson, a hard man with a "love 'em and leave 'em" reputation, had fallen head over heels in love.

"Well, I'll be damned," he said aloud, not nearly so afraid of the emotion as he'd thought would be the case.

"Very likely," Adam agreed, strolling into the room. "What's condemned you to hell on this particular occasion?"

"I think I've met my match in Porcha," he admitted sheepishly. "Never felt this way before."

He expected Adam to guffaw. Instead he merely shook his head and smiled. "You and me both, buddy. Beck, too, I shouldn't wonder. We can't let her go."

"She might not want to stay."

Adam's grin was positively lethal. "Then we'll just have to persuade her, won't we?"

"Persuade who to do what?" Beck asked as he joined them.

"Porcha not to go back to England."

"She's not going anywhere," Beck said with absolute certainty. "She's staying right here with us, where she belongs."

The three guys shared high clenched fists, just as a naked Porcha walked into the kitchen.

"What are you celebrating?" she asked.

All three of them ran their eyes down the length of her body and grinned.

"We're celebrating having you, darlin'," Troy told her, pulling out a chair for her at the kitchen table.

"You have *the* most amazing tits," Beck told her, sitting across from her and ogling them shamelessly. "I could look at them all day."

"You have been," Adam reminded him.

"Just sayin'."

"Thank you, sir."

Adam grinned. "And if we get tired of looking at the tits, there's always those legs and that cute butt to offer us a different view."

"There's something about having a beautiful, naked woman sitting at the table that gives me an appetite." Troy took a healthy bite of his tuna-and-mayo sandwich to prove his point.

"Eat up, Porcha." Adam held a sandwich to her lips. "You need to keep your strength up. Troy's got plans for us all tonight that will require stamina."

"Oh no, I'm so sorry!"

"What is it, sweetheart?" they all asked together.

"You got me excited, and I just leaked all over the chair."

The three men roared with laughter.

"Doesn't take much to excite you, does it?" Adam remarked.

"If you think that your three cocks aren't much, then I guess I'd have to agree."

"Well, Adam's might not be much to write home about," Beck said, grinning, "but I'm packing a huge woody right this very moment."

"Keep it in your pants," Troy told him curtly. "Our little sub needs to get some rest this afternoon so she can service us all later."

"I can wait," Beck said, fingering his prick through his shorts. "I can wait 'cause I know it'll be worth waiting for."

As soon as lunch was cleared away, Troy took them all into the study and told them he'd decided to go ahead with the e-mail to Georgio.

"The way I see it," he said, leaning back in his chair, "is that Sal went to Mexico with Woollard and we don't know who else and got knocked off. Whether or not Woollard's still alive is uncertain. Whether he was involved in setting his boss up is another unknown. Porcha saw her home overrun with gunmen who might have been looking for her or something she possesses. Either way, *someone's* out to get her, and I don't intend to sit back and wait for that someone to come to us."

"Glad to hear it," Beck said.

Adam nodded. "Me, too."

"If Woollard's alive then he's either a hero or the villain of the piece." Troy paused. "The limited information we have points to the latter."

"I agree," Beck said.

"But we don't even know if Woollard got out of Mexico alive," Adam pointed out. "We're just assuming he's behind all this."

"More an educated guess," Troy said. "I never make assumptions."

"I could ring the house and ask for him," Porcha said. "And then hang up if they said they were going to get him."

"No, I'd rather you didn't. They'd recognize your voice. One of us could make the call, but I already rang the guardroom without a valid reason. I suspect that both the house and guardroom numbers aren't in general circulation." Porcha nodded. "Well then, if Woollard is alive he'll have been told about the bogus call to the guardhouse. If you call the house as well, it'll alert him that we're up to something."

"I suppose."

"I think we should call anyway," Adam said. "It's ridiculous setting up a campaign against a man when we don't even know if he's in the country."

Troy grimaced. "Yeah, you're right. What's the house number, babe?"

She told him. Troy picked up the secure line, dialed the number, and asked for Woollard when it was answered.

"A friend of Mrs. Gonzalez's," he said, presumably when asked who was calling.

Troy hung up. "They were going to get him," he said.

"Well," Beck said cheerfully. "At least we know now who we're up against."

"What we know," Troy said, "is that Woollard went to Mexico with his boss. That boss got whacked, but Woollard came back, presumably unscathed, and took over Sal's operation."

"Looks that way," Adam and Beck said together.

"I spoke to Georgio whilst Adam and Porcha were playing earlier, and he knows what we're doing." Troy clicked a few keys and a laptop screen sprang into life. "This is what I think Porcha should say in her initial contact."

They all peered at the screen, nodding their approval.

"I've said that she'll be meeting her contact at that particular mall because it's small, out of the way, and easy for the three of us to cover if we get there far enough in advance. It doesn't get a lot of traffic, so if things get nasty, the likelihood of any passersby getting caught in the cross fire is remote."

"Will our reputations ever recover?" Beck asked, acting the fool as usual. "You're encouraging this gorgeous creature to pretend that she's immune to our charms. Once her words are committed to cyberspace, there's no pulling 'em back."

"You don't have any charm," Adam pointed out.

"Don't need it with what I've got here," he responded, grabbing his groin.

"Shut it, you two." Troy waved a hand at them. "What do you think, Porcha? Still wanna do this?"

"Absolutely!"

"Okay, turn your iPad on. This will need to go from your account, obviously."

Once she'd logged on, Troy quickly transferred the message to an e-mail from her address and pressed send.

"Now then, we're going to teach you a few more things about taking care of yourself that you might not already know," Troy told her.

"We always plan for the best but prepare for the worst," Adam added.

"If we've missed something vital and you get taken and held," Beck said, "there's almost always some way out, or something to help you defend yourself, if you know what you're looking for."

For the next hour they drilled stuff into her head. Porcha was a quick study and seldom needed to be told anything twice.

"Of course," Troy said. "The easiest way out of any locked room is simply to pick the lock. Ever tried it?"

"No. They make it look easy on films, just running a credit card along the slot and it magically opens."

"Can't rely on having a credit card on hand, but these little babies are easy to conceal." Troy flashed a lockpick beneath her nose.

"So are these." Adam waved another tiny gadget at her. "Small but ever so tough."

"You could slip both inside your bra and no one would ever notice," Beck said, grinning. "What's a little extra weight when you're already packing so much?"

"We're serious about this, Porcha," Troy said. "Come on, I'll give you a beginner's course in lock picking."

Half an hour later she had it down pat and was able to open a lock blindfolded.

"Not quite the situation I had in mind for a blindfold," Beck said, "but I guess it's a start."

"Okay, that should do it."

A screen flashed to tell Troy that he had an e-mail.

"It's from Georgio," he said, clicking on it. "I asked him to see what he could find out about Woollard."

Troy read quickly. "Ben Woollard is twenty-eight and has been Sal's right-hand man for eight years, completely loyal, hard as nails, blah, blah. That jibes with what you told us, Porcha."

"Present whereabouts unknown," Beck read over Troy's shoulder. "Fat lot of fucking good that is."

Troy clicked on the attachment and a picture of a fit-looking guy with close-cropped blond hair filled the screen. "That him?"

"Yes." Porcha shuddered. "That's the creep."

"Well, at least we know now who we're looking for," Adam said. "Presumably, he'll turn up in person."

"Time will tell," Troy said grimly. "Porcha, go and get some rest. We've got stuff to do, and then Adam's gonna cook us a feast to prepare us for the games to come." Troy placed an arm round her bare shoulders and dropped a kiss on the top of her head. "I'll come and wake you in a couple of hours with the clothes we want you to wear at dinner."

She dropped her eyes when he made it obvious that his mind was no longer on the battle with Woollard but games of a very different nature. She looked indescribably endearing as she submitted to him so instinctively. Troy somehow resisted the urge to bend her over his desk and fuck...No, not fuck. He was amazed to discover that his feelings were tender. He wanted to make love to her—give her every possible pleasure, mindless of his own needs—right here amongst his precious computer screens, for the rest of the afternoon. Troy *never* made love. He fucked, pure and simple. What the hell was she doing to him? To them all?

"Yes, masters," she said, turning on her heel and heading for the stairs.

All three of them watched her cute ass until it disappeared from view.

"Geez, she's killing us," Beck said for them all, running his hand through his hair and expelling a long sigh of frustration.

* * * *

Troy surfed through a dozen incoming e-mails, turning down two potential jobs without referring them to the others. Whilst they worked for Georgio a lot of the time, they also freelanced, picking and choosing their assignments because they were the best, much in demand, but didn't need the money.

"Christ, a spoiled rich kid needs protecting." He turned up his nose and deleted the proposed assignment without bothering to respond. "What the hell do these people think we are? Fucking nursemaids?"

Adam was taking his turn in the gym, and Beck was sprawled on a couch, reading a political biography. Anyone who didn't know him well tended to think he was an airhead, which was precisely what he wanted them to think. But Beck was at least as smart as the rest of them. He certainly pulled his weight in the crew, even if he was sometimes a bit of a hothead.

Troy smiled as he thought of the tussles he'd had with him and Adam in the early days when they were all raw conscripts in the same unit, vying for supremacy. Even then, Troy realized now, there'd been a degree of inevitability about their future—almost like they'd been thrown together for a reason. They were from different backgrounds, different cultures even, but they gelled for all that, complementing one another's strengths and protecting one another's backs in tight situations without the need to be asked. That had never changed over the years, nor would it.

But a permanent woman in their organized existence? Would it work? Troy flexed his jaw. Hell, the way he felt right now it would damned well have to, because he had no intention of letting Porcha get away from him.

The time passed quickly, and when Adam reappeared to start prepping his gourmet meal, Troy went to wake Porcha.

Beck wagged a finger at him as he left the lounge. "No sneaking a quickie."

"Wouldn't dream of it." Troy grinned. "Half the fun is making her wait until she begs for it."

Beck returned his grin. "Ain't that the truth."

Troy let himself into Porcha's room without knocking.

She appeared to be sound asleep, but Troy wasn't taking any chances. He had no intention of sitting on the bed and being coerced into it by the sexy little witch who didn't seem to be able to get enough of any of them.

"Wake up, Porcha," he said authoritatively.

She sat up immediately, confirming that she'd been awake all the time. The cover slipped from her tits, and he was hard-pressed to contain a groan. His cock was rigid. Nothing new there. He'd been in a permanent state of arousal ever since he'd met her.

"Get up."

She threw back the covers and stood naked in front of him.

"Put this on."

He handed her the garment he wanted her to wear but didn't help her with it. Without hesitating, she stepped into the tight black PVC dress with thin shoulder straps and a hemline that barely cleared her ass.

"Christ!"

She looked spectacular. The top was too tight for her tits, and they spilled out of the cups. There were lace panels down the front, back, and sides of the dress, and it was so short that the cheeks of her ass were apparent every time she moved.

"Something wrong, master?" she asked, a little too innocently.

"Absolutely nothing." He cleared his throat. "I have something else for you. Something that you'll wear all the time while in this house if you're comfortable with it." He fastened a studded collar round her neck. "Put these on as well."

He handed her a pair of strappy shoes with four-inch heels. She sat on the edge of the bed, slipped her feet into them, and fastened them in place.

"Take a look at yourself."

He held out a hand to her and led her to the full-length mirror. She gasped when she saw herself, which was hardly surprising. She was the sexiest goddamned woman he'd ever seen. She even managed to make tacky PVC look classy. He wondered if she saw herself in the same light, wondered if the clothing made her feel as sexy as she looked. Her green eyes sparkled with anticipation, her tousled hair fell all over her shoulders, and her nipples pushed against the fabric of the dress, the tops of her aureoles spilling out as though they couldn't stand being covered up. They didn't need to worry. It wouldn't be for long.

"What do you think?" he asked, grasping her shoulders from behind.

"What I think doesn't matter. I want you to be pleased with me, master."

Troy chuckled. "I think I can promise you that all three of us will be pleased to have you at our table tonight. In fact," he added, dropping his head and nuzzling her ear, "you might well finish up being the main course." He led her away from the mirror. "Lean over the bed and stick your ass in the air. I have something else for you."

She did as he asked, and Troy applied a generous dollop of lube to the crack in her ass, working it into her anus with one finger. As soon as she was slick, he inserted a butt plug, pushing it all the way home, helped by Porcha, who pushed against it and sighed when she'd taken it all.

"Stand up and squeeze your ass cheeks together." He could see that she did as he asked. "It's full of oil that will heat up inside you and drive you wild. It'll also dilate you enough for what we plan to do to you later."

Porcha licked her lips and smiled but, well-trained sub that she was, asked no questions.

"That dress." He shook his head. "I was gonna save these for later, but they seem kinda appropriate." He delved into his bag and produced clover nipple clamps attached to one another by a chain. "Come here."

She stepped up to him, and Troy pushed the flimsy fabric away from first one nipple and then the other, attaching the clamps to the accompaniment of soft sighs from Porcha. He pulled the fabric back in place when he was done, knowing it would rub against her hardened, sensitized nipples and really turn her on.

"Like that?"

"Hmm, it's heavenly."

"It's gonna get a bit rough tonight, Porcha, but you do know you can call a halt any time you like?" He reached out to touch her and abruptly pulled his hand back again. If he touched her just once he'd end up shagging her. That's how desperate she made him, especially the way she looked right now in her tarty clothing, her nipples clamped, his plug up her ass, their collar round her neck…Fuck it, he wanted her so much he could barely think straight.

"Don't bail on me, Troy. I love all this stuff. I love the way the three of you look at me. How your cocks stand to attention whenever I'm around." She smiled. "I'm submitting to you, but when I see what I do to you, I feel as though I'm the one in control."

How right she is! "Just so long as you're completely sure."

"Absolutely, completely sure."

Troy wrapped her in his arms and kissed her with tenderness. "I'm so glad," he said, smiling into her eyes when he finally released her.

"Okay, I'm going downstairs now. Wait until I call and then walk down slowly. I want the others to get a real eyeful."

"Yes, master."

Chapter Eleven

Porcha ran a brush through her tangled mane of hair whilst she waited to be summoned, her lips burning from the searing passion of Troy's kiss. She was so excited about the night to come that her fingers could barely grip the brush. She glanced at her reflection and almost didn't recognize herself. The flushed face, the gleam of anticipation in her eye, the sexy clothing, the nipple clamps, the plug heating in her butt—she was so damned turned-on that she was tempted to do something about it then and there.

"Get a grip!" she said aloud. "They'll know, and it won't please them."

And Porcha definitely wanted to please her three masters. Their games were a hundred times removed from the humiliations she'd suffered at Sal's hands. He wanted to possess her, to own her, to make her grovel before him in public because he had some sort of twisted point to prove.

Troy, Beck, and Adam wanted to love her, to give pleasure in return for receiving it, and would never intentionally hurt her or cause her embarrassment. She hadn't known them for long but already trusted them implicitly. They wanted to play as hard as they worked, and who was she to object when all three of them seemed so intensely focused on her? Doubts about her ability to hold their interest filtered through her brain, but she shut them out. Failure simply wasn't an option. She could do this! She *wanted* to do it. No one controlled her head anymore, and she was free to please herself.

"It's time, Porcha."

Troy's softly spoken command intruded on her introspective thoughts. Her pulse rate increased as she prepared to make her entrance, hoping her lovers would like what they saw. If they reacted true to form, she'd be confronted with three rock-hard cocks primed and ready for action. Hell, her pussy was leaking already, just at the thought of it. She dashed into the bathroom and cleaned herself up, then tossed her head back, winked at her reflection, and left the room.

"I'm coming, masters," she said in a sultry voice.

"You'd better not be until we say you can!"

Beck, of course. Always the joker. Except she guessed he wasn't joking about this. Porcha really would have to try and find a little discipline and keep her impulses in check. Problem was, their taunting, the way in which they took her to the brink only to hold back and forbid her to come until they said she could, was exquisite agony. She'd never known anything that came close to the thrill she got from submitting to them but didn't think she'd ever be able to match their level of control.

She set one high-heeled foot on the top step, grasped the bannister for support, and walked down the stairs slowly, aware that they'd have a perfect view of her naked pussy from beneath the open slats. A collective intake of male breath told her they were taking a good long look.

"Fuck it, Troy, what have you done to her?" Adam asked.

"Who gives a shit *how* he did it," Beck answered. "Let's just make the most of the results."

Adam dropped his chin into his cupped hand, watching her as she slowly made her way to join them. "She got a plug in her butt?"

"Yep."

"Thought so." The men continued to discuss her as though she couldn't hear them. "You can always tell by the way they walk with their ass cheeks squeezed together."

Porcha reached the ground floor and stopped at the bottom of the stairs. She deliberately made eye contact with each of them, which would probably get her spanked, and then dropped her gaze to the floor, waiting to be told what to do next. She could see that they all wanted to step forward and touch her, but none of them did.

"Sit in the swivel chair by the window," Troy said.

Porcha sashayed her way to the chair in question and sat down, knees primly pressed together. Her nipples ached from the pressure of the clamps, but pleasantly so, the fabric of her skimpy dress rubbing against them and sending fine tremors of expectancy lancing through her. All three men stood a little way away from her. Troy leaned against the mantelpiece, Adam and Beck flanking him, their gazes focused on her like they'd never seen her before.

"Guess it's cocktail time."

Adam went into the kitchen and returned with a chilled bottle of champagne. Popping the cork without spilling a single drop, he poured the wine into four flutes and handed one to Porcha.

"You comfortable, babe?" Troy asked.

"Yes…well, no but—"

"What do you need?" Beck asked.

To be fucked senseless. "To please you three gentlemen."

Beck chuckled. "Well trained, ain't she?"

"She's a shameless little cock tease who's gonna have that cute little backside thoroughly spanked before the night's out," Troy said like he meant it.

Adam pursed his lips. "Ask me, that won't be much of a punishment, given the sparkle you've just put in her eye."

"Ah, but you guys know what else we have in store for her." Troy finally turned to include Porcha in a discussion that involved her but to which she hadn't been invited to contribute until then. "We all have different things we like to do, and tonight we're gonna do them." He grinned at her. "To you."

"Multiple times," Beck added.

"Thank you."

"And you're gonna love what we do with our cocks, how we punish you, how we chain you down and make you beg for it." Troy winked at her. "Count on it."

Porcha was, and judging by the bulges in their pants, she was pretty sure she wouldn't be disappointed.

"We need to eat first."

Adam disappeared into the kitchen again and reappeared with plates of appetizers that he placed on the dining table.

"We're set," he said.

Porcha knew better than to move until she was given permission.

"Over here," Troy said, holding a chair out for her.

The plug in her butt was now so warm that her ass felt like it was on fire. It was almost but not quite painful, but Porcha didn't say so, just in case Troy decided to punish her by taking it away. She sat down carefully in the chair he held out for her.

"Any interesting offers come in?" Adam asked Troy as they made inroads into their grilled vegetables.

"Nah. Nothing worthy of our talents."

"More babysitting assignments?" Beck asked, wrinkling his nose.

"I declined them all." Troy stretched his arms above his head. "I guess we'll be on vacation after this, until something interesting comes along."

"I hate vacations," Beck complained.

"Depends who you spend 'em with." Adam's gaze lingered on Porcha like he wanted to eat her instead of the delicious food he'd prepared for them. "I can think of no end of interesting ways to pass the time with this little firecracker."

Beck nodded. "Well, there is that, I guess."

The main course came and went, and not one of them had addressed a single comment to her. But their gazes were constantly on her, seeming to assess her mood, waiting for the right moment to start the party. Being ignored verbally and simultaneously fucked with their eyes wasn't a situation she'd have expected to find particularly exciting. How wrong could she be? The dark weight of Troy's gaze that promised so much, the smouldering luminescence in Adam's eye, Becks candid appraisal of every inch of her—three different approaches that made her burn with impatience. The desire to get on with things, engendered merely by the killer grin tugging at Troy's lips one moment, the flicker of heat in Beck's eye the next, was making her crazy. She guessed that was kind of the point. Damn, they were good at what they did, and the games hadn't even started yet.

Porcha, her mind free to wander, looked at the three of them as they chatted about places and things she knew nothing about. They were so goddamned handsome that it took her breath away just to look at them. She wanted to pinch herself, just to be sure that she really was here and was about to have all three of them—probably multiple times. The plug in her butt felt as though it was getting hotter, keeping pace with her thoughts. *Come on, guys, I'm in pain here.*

To take her mind off her desperation, Porcha assessed each of them in turn, still marveling at her good fortune. Troy with his swarthy Argentinian complexion and thick black hair tied back in a ponytail. Beck with his open features, brown hair, and gray eyes that always had a smile in them. Adam with his blond surfer-boy good looks and iron control. They were all hers, at least for now, and she felt deep affection for each of them in different ways.

Was it possible to love three men equally? Presumably so, because love was what she felt for these compassionate hunks. No question. Love and appreciation for the care they took of her overcame even her raging desire to be fucked. She toyed with her food, willing to play them at their own game, ready to wait. She had a feeling that the waiting was getting to them, too, and that they weren't nearly as in control now as they had been when she came downstairs. The waiting wouldn't drag on for much longer.

"Okay, guys, time to rock."

Troy pushed his chair back, the cue for the other two to stand as well. Porcha stayed where she was, waiting to be told what to do.

"Okay, Porcha, you can stand up."

Beck attached a long chain to the front of her collar and led her toward the stairs. Troy and Adam walked behind her, still chatting casually as though it was the most normal thing in the world for Beck to lead a scantily clad woman wearing nipple clamps and with a plug up her butt along by a chain. In this household, it probably was. Porcha tried not to feel jealous as she wondered about the women they'd played with before her. All that mattered now was that she was the subject of their attentions, and she was damned if they'd find her wanting. Aware that her problems would be resolved one way or another within the next few days and that she wouldn't see them again after that, Porcha fully intended to make the most of them whilst she still could.

They climbed the two flights of stairs in silence. When they reached the playroom, Beck opened the door and led her through it. Once inside, he shed what few clothes he was wearing and sat on the edge of the bed.

"On your knees," he told her curtly.

Porcha knelt in front of him, eyes downcast. Beck obviously got to go first, which was fine by Porcha. She tried to anticipate what he might require of her. Then she recalled that she'd tossed him on his butt that morning. Men like Beck didn't let things like that go unpunished. She stifled a giggle. Of course his revenge would be dramatic and oversized, just like everything else about him, especially his cock.

"You like to wrestle, sweetheart?"

"If it pleases you."

He chuckled. "Oh, it does. I aim to pin you down every which way this side of Christmas and fuck you senseless. But first you need to be chastised for what you did this morning."

"I was wrong, master. I need to be punished." She lifted her gaze to his face. "Please punish me."

Porcha was aware of Troy and Adam in the periphery of her vision, both now naked and sitting together on a sofa as they watched Beck in action. Having them as an audience was a thousand times different from the way she had felt with Sal and his business connections. That was humiliating because they were a captive audience, didn't necessarily want to be there, and certainly couldn't participate. But they stayed because they didn't dare to go against Sal's wishes and probably thought she was a first-class tart for doing what he made her do.

This, on the other hand, was red hot.

"How would you like to be punished?"

"That's for you to decide."

Beck tapped her thigh. "I asked you a question. Tell me what you want."

Porcha licked her lips, her eyes focused on his massive erection. "Your cock deep inside me."

"Ah-hah." Beck wagged a finger beneath her nose. "Not yet, babe. We need to let you know who's the boss here first."

He attached the chain to a hook on the side of the bed. "On your hands and knees."

Porcha moved into position, aware that her dress—what little there was of it—had ridden up to completely expose her ass. Troy and Adam would have an up-close view, and she cheekily waggled her butt in their direction. Muffled chuckles confirmed that they'd got the message.

"She's getting out of line again, Beck," Troy said.

"Yeah, I got that."

She couldn't see what Beck was doing but heard more rattling and then felt cuffs being placed round her ankles, also presumably attached to the side of the bed.

"Spread your legs wider," Beck said in a gruff voice.

Porcha moved them as far apart as the chain attaching the leg restraints would allow. Without warning, it went dark when he fixed a blindfold over her eyes.

"Now you're completely at my mercy!" She felt his hair brush the side of her face as he leaned in close. "Do you like being chained here with your ass exposed, waiting for my punishment?"

Porcha swallowed against the lump that had formed in her throat. "Very much."

Beck chuckled. "Yeah, I can tell."

He brought a switch down across her ass, gently the first time. Not expecting it, Porcha flinched, the sting it left behind very slight and not nearly enough to satisfy her raging desire to be whipped. Anticipating the second blow as she heard the switch make a soft whoosh in the air, she relaxed her muscles and rolled with the pain. In combination with the red-hot plug in her butt, it felt wonderfully sensual, and she softly moaned her appreciation.

"You've been a very bad girl, Porcha."

"I'm sorry, master."

She felt something slip into her pussy and disappear. A vibrator, switched to a low speed. Porcha was now in some difficulty. She could imagine how she must look, sluttish clothing, chained hand and foot, blindfolded, and with vibrators back and front—not to mention the nipple clamps that were now giving her merry hell. She was ready to come then and there. In fact she was desperate to do so.

"What do you want now, Porcha?" Beck's whispered the question in her ear.

"To be fucked, if that's what you'd like."

"Well now, I don't think that's gonna happen," he said teasingly.

She sensed him moving away from her and quelled her disappointment. His hair brushed against her face again, and she realized that he'd slipped beneath her when he forced his rigid cock between her lips.

"There's only one person gonna come right now, and it ain't you, baby. Eat it!" She dutifully sucked him into her month, taking him right to the back of her throat. "You really shouldn't have put me on my ass," he said censoriously. "Hey, that's it, suck it deeper, darlin'. Eat my cock." When she felt his hand pumping it deeper into her mouth she reached for his balls, exerting enough pressure on them to make him gasp. "Christ, this is gonna be quick. Suck it deeper, sweetheart. Come on, I'm fucking your mouth. You feel that? Milk it for me, babe."

Porcha was turned-on by his words as much as by the butt plug and vibrator still pumping away inside her pussy. If she just closed her legs a little—he'd never notice—she'd be able to rub her thighs together and make herself come. She moaned softly round Beck's cock, *so* needing to come.

"Stop it!"

A sharp tap on her butt told her that Troy or Adam knew what she was trying to do. She stilled immediately, widening her legs again as she worked on Beck, and felt a finger push the plug a little deeper. Beck was panting with need, and when she felt him pulsate and expand a little more in her mouth, she knew he was close.

"That's it. I'm fucking your mouth, Porcha. I'm fucking that sweet mouth real good. Swallow it down deep, babe. Here it comes!"

Groaning, he shot an endless stream of semen deep into her throat. Porcha swallowed it all and wiped her mouth with the back of her hand when his cum finally stopped spurting. As soon as he slipped out of her mouth he removed the blindfold, smiling as he wiped himself clean and dropped a kiss on her lips.

"Let that be a lesson to you."

"Thank you, master."

Chapter Twelve

"Let the chains go from the side of the bed but leave them on her," Troy said, standing up.

Adam stood with him, watching as Beck released their willing little sub. "That was quite a show," he said.

"Not bad for a prologue."

"How was it, Porcha?" Adam asked.

"Frustrating," she responded with a mischievous little smile.

"I'll just bet it was, but then that was the idea. You really shouldn't try to get the better of Beck." Adam wagged a finger beneath her nose. "He doesn't much like being fooled with."

"Sorry, master Beck," she said contritely.

"In his situation, I wouldn't have let you get away so lightly," Adam told her.

Troy chuckled as he looked at Porcha, now standing with the chain dangling from her collar and her legs still cuffed. They'd withheld what she most wanted for too long, he could tell that much by the rebellious expression in her eye, and because she'd just dared to admit it. If they didn't give it to her soon, she'd find a way to get off on her own, not caring—or probably hoping—to be punished for her disobedience.

Troy flashed a grin at Adam. Time to give her just a little bit more. He sat on the edge of the bed, snagging her waist and pulling her down with him, the lightweight chains rattling as she landed on his lap. He reached up and pulled the band out of his hair, feeling it cascade about his shoulders as soon as it was liberated. Porcha reached up and ran her fingers through it.

"Just so you know, Porcha, he means business when he literally lets his hair down," Adam said, chuckling. "You might be in for a rough ride."

"I'd better be."

* * * *

The other two laughed as Troy reached up, cupped the back of her neck, and kissed her. His lips were as hard as the rest of him, crushing her mouth as he demanded and instantly received her complete capitulation. Her clamped nipples crashed against his chest as he held her closer and deepened the kiss. As his tongue foraged her mouth and his teeth nipped playfully at her lower lip, he felt himself drowning in her femininity and wondered who was actually in charge here. She was a goddamned witch. A drug he'd never be able to get enough of. That didn't mean he wouldn't spend every spare moment he had getting his fill of her.

"Get on your hands and knees in the middle of the bed."

She did as she asked, panting with need. Troy slid beneath her, disciplining himself not to touch her tits yet as he removed the vibrator and flicked at her soaking pussy with the tip of his tongue. She moaned as she dropped her hips so that her clit fell directly over his face. Smiling at her desperation, Troy sank his lips into her most sensitive area and sucked the life out of her.

"Troy!"

He let go, grinning as he imagined her annoyance at having spoken his name and making him stop so he could answer her. "Yes, babe, what is it?"

"Please." She brushed her pubic bone over his face. "I need you to do that some more."

"You want me to suck your cunt?"

"Very badly."

"You know what happens to girls who ask?" Beck questioned sternly.

"I'm not asking, master, I'm begging." She was almost crying with need. "I'll do anything if you'll just—"

"You'll do anything anyway."

Troy brought one hand down hard across her ass as he resumed feasting on her clit. She bucked into his mouth, whimpering. It clearly wasn't enough for her but was all she was gonna get—for now, anyway. His tongue delved deep into her pussy, licking her walls, sucking her lips, while the fingers of one hand found her clit. It was all it took.

"Master, I can't...oh God, I'm going to come!"

And she did, bucking, screaming, pushing so hard down on his mouth that Troy almost drew blood as he sucked the orgasm out of her. When she finally stopped moving, he slid out from beneath her, twisted her onto her back, and flopped down beside her, trying not to laugh at the relief in her expression.

"Better?"

"Yes, thank you. Do you want to punish me now?"

"Oh, I've got something a little more interesting than a straightforward punishment in mind for you."

Troy stood up, extended one hand, and pulled her to her feet.

"Your body's pretty supple from all that self-defense shit, right?"

"Yes, master."

"Ever used a strappado?"

"No. What is it?"

"It used to be a form of torture back in the dark ages. Now it's part of the bondage scene and when used properly gives unbelievable pleasure, just so long as you're young and supple and do as you're told. Wanna try it?"

"Absolutely!"

Her enthusiasm for the unknown knocked a further dent in Troy's already-vulnerable heart. Part of him wanted to fold her protectively in his arms and never let her anywhere near his strappado. What if he got it wrong and injured her? He wouldn't be able to live with himself if that happened. But the anticipation shining from her eyes, her eagerness to get started, and his desperation to try this gizmo with the woman who'd stolen his heart overcame common sense.

"Remember, babe," he said, holding her close as he helped her walk across the room in her leg restraints. "If it gets to be too much, call a halt and I'll stop immediately. The last thing I want to do is hurt you."

"Nothing you do to me will ever hurt." She lifted a hand and ran it down the curve of his face, the gesture assured and profoundly sensual. "All you ever do is make me horny as hell."

Adam and Beck laughed.

"I do admire honesty in a woman," Beck said.

Troy kissed her shoulder and ran a hand across her backside, satisfied that she knew what she was getting into and was willing to play. The day had yet to dawn when he'd force a woman do anything that made her uncomfortable—especially this woman.

Once they reached the opposite wall, Troy fastened cuffs to her wrists.

"Reach your arms up, babe. They're gonna be attached to that hook up there, which will pull them back and up over your shoulders. That could be uncomfortable, but these are suspension cuffs, and you can hold that bar right there."

She mangled her lower lip between her teeth as she considered his proposition. "That's cool," she said without hesitation.

"Her flexibility is giving me all sorts of ideas," Beck remarked.

Adam rolled his eyes. "Everything gives you ideas."

"You have to admit, though, she's one hell of an athlete."

"Okay, if you're sure, let's do it." Troy hooked her arms above her. "All right?"

"Fine."

"Now bend forward and open your legs. The chain from the collar gets attached to the chain separating the leg restraints so your cute ass it bent up for me and I can fuck it standing behind you."

"Oh!"

He caressed her buttocks with one hand. "Yeah, oh."

All three of the guys sucked in deep, appreciative breaths at the sight of her. Troy had never found anyone who could do this without experiencing extreme discomfort and had always called a halt before it got underway. Porcha appeared to love it, and it was obvious from the way she wiggled her ass at him that she felt only excitement. He walked up behind her and slapped her backside, at the same time removing the butt plug. It slid out, accompanied by a stream of her juices that soaked the floor.

"Naughty, naughty!" Troy reached forward to smack her cunt, at the same time running his rigid cock down the crease in her butt. "What do you feel, babe?"

"Your massive cock, master." She sighed. "Am I allowed to tell you that I love your cock, especially when it's as big as it is right now?"

"You're a greedy little madam who can't get enough pricks inside you." He leaned over her back, squinting at her face, anxious to ensure that she wasn't in pain. Her expression *was* pained, but Troy reckoned that was more a case of anticipation than any actual discomfort. With her torso pulled backward, the nipple clamps must have tightened even more. He pushed the straps from her shoulders and revealed her breasts, the nipples red and angry from the clamps. He ran his tongue over one of them and received a soft moan for his trouble. "Like that?"

"God yes!"

"Not too tight?"

"Stop worrying."

"You really do like our cocks, isn't that right, Porcha?" he said softly, continuing to rub his against her ass. "You'd have the three of us fucking you all day and all night, given half the chance."

"Yes, master." She sobbed the words. "I can't think about anything else when you guys are near me."

"Glad we got that one sorted," Beck said, fisting his erection like he meant business.

Troy grabbed Porcha round the waist and pulled her toward him, stretching her arms a little in the opposite direction.

"This is an exercise in discipline," he whispered. "Spread your legs as wide as they'll go for balance, and then you have to stand absolutely still and let me fuck you. If you move you'll hurt yourself."

"Absolutely still?"

"Completely still. Don't move a muscle." He ran a possessive hand over her thigh. "You ready to do this, babe?"

"Yes."

"Then tell me what you want me to do to you. I need to hear you say it."

"I want you to fuck me whilst I stay chained up and don't move a muscle."

Troy brushed his lips down the length of her neck. "Think you can do that?"

"Yes, just don't make me wait too long for it."

Troy chuckled. "Wouldn't think of it."

He rubbed his slick cock around her anus and slid into her. They both moaned as it went deep, meeting no resistance. He sensed Porcha's muscles bunching, as though she was about to move. He reached one hand round her front and tapped her pussy again, harder this time.

"Keep absolutely still. Let me do the work."

Troy started to move inside her, one hand still holding her firmly by the waist, the other playing with a clamped nipple.

"Look up, Porcha. Look at yourself in the mirror. It's just about the sexiest damned thing I've ever seen."

"You've got that right," Adam agreed. He and Beck were now both playing with their erections.

Porcha lifted her eyes and gasped. She'd obviously forgotten about the large mirror on the wall opposite. Either that or she'd been too excited to even notice it. He wondered if she saw herself as the rest of them did. There was something about a woman in restraints, her arms pulled backward behind her head, pushing her large tits even farther in front of her that absolutely did it for Troy. He sank deeper into her, increasing the speed and ferocity of his thrusts.

"Stop it!"

He could sense from her increasingly frantic moans that she was close to orgasm. He wanted her to come. He wanted to hear her scream his name and beg to be fucked harder. The best way to make that happen was to forbid it. Sure enough, words spilled from her lips, and she only just managed to remain still, pushing her butt just a little toward him each time he rammed into her.

"Troy, I can't...I—geez." She tossed her head to one side and screamed. "I can't hold it. Fuck me, Troy! Give it to me hard."

Murmurs from the other two told Troy that they were having a hard time just watching. Troy stayed with Porcha as she spasmed against him, only just stopping himself from shooting his load. When she finally stopped trembling, he picked up the pace again and slammed into her, his balls slapping against her backside as he let himself go.

"Here it is, Porcha. You're making me crazy. Let's come together, babe. Come on, do you feel me?"

"Yes, I feel it. I'm coming again. God, I love this position! I love feeling helpless. At your complete mercy. Fuck me again, Troy. Make me yours."

"I'm fucking you as hard as I can, baby."

Troy yelled with triumph as he shot an endless stream of his sperm into Porcha's backside. The noise he made was trumped by Porcha's screams as she came a second time, moving as much as she dared against the chains that kept her head bent forward but her arms stretched back. If it hurt, she didn't seem to either know or care.

As soon as they were both spent, Troy released her and massaged her upper arms, taking off the handcuffs and nipple clamps.

"Aw!"

"You've had enough of those for now." Troy laughed as he trailed kisses down her shoulder and onto a liberated nipple. "I was going to ask if you're okay, but I think you just answered my question." He shook his head, making no effort to conceal the admiration he felt for her. "You were absolutely amazing."

"If felt fabulous." She smiled radiantly. "My arms ache a bit, but I'm not hurt, and you were right, it's a great way to exercise restraint." Porcha nibbled playfully at her lower lip. "As you know by now, I'm not big on restraint. Can we do it again?"

All three men roared with laughter, and they shook their heads in admiration.

"Adam decides on the next game," Troy said, releasing her leg restraints and leading her back to the bed.

Chapter Thirteen

"May I visit the bathroom?"

Troy smiled at her. "Take all the time you need, babe."

Porcha took him at his word. Once she'd wiped herself clean she perched on the edge of the tub and thought about what she'd just done. She was no novice when it came to sex games—how could she be after a three-year marriage to Sal?—but these guys took playtime to a whole new level. Not that she was complaining. Troy's strappy thing was a blast, but she was far from done. She wanted more from all three of them. A whole lot more. What would Adam's preference be? She tilted her head as she thought about it, but nothing obvious sprang to mind.

"Adam's ready for you," Beck said, poking his head round the door. "Don't keep him waiting."

"I'll be right there."

When she walked back to the loft, she discovered that the bed had been covered with a waterproof sheet. Interesting. She was obviously going to get wet.

"What would you like me to do for you, master?" she asked, stopping directly in front of Adam and adopting a subservient pose.

"There's a question you don't hear from a beautiful woman every day," Beck remarked, chuckling.

Adam took her hand and led her to the bed.

"Lay down right in the middle, arms out to the side." He fastened them to underbed restraints as soon as she was in place. "I'd prefer them above your head, but I don't think that's a good idea, not after the way Troy just make you hold them up for so long."

"Thank you."

Adam ran a finger so gently round one of her aureoles that she thought at first she'd imagined the contact. It was almost more erotic than the rough handling she'd received from Troy. Hard and soft, demanding or taunting—Porcha liked both. Her body was certainly reacting to Adam's soft form of torture with almost embarrassing enthusiasm. Except she had nothing to be embarrassed about. She was supposed to be turned-on by what they did to her. They wanted to make her squirm, and there was no reason she could think of to hide her reaction.

She pushed herself into his hand, greedy for more, glanced down, and noticed he was using a feather. It tickled and teased its way down her body, pausing at her pussy but not actually touching it, sending tingles of anticipation spiralling through her entire nervous system. She was surprised by the extent of the desperate need she felt to have Adam inside her so soon after being thoroughly fucked by Troy. The small part of her brain still capable of rational thought wondered why they needed a plastic sheet if this was all he intended to do, but if she asked, Adam might stop using that feather, just to punish her. She wasn't prepared to take the chance.

Adam replaced the feather with his lips. He started at her mouth, kissing her with tenderness and controlled passion as his tongue tickled playfully at the corners of her mouth. Then he trailed down the column of her neck, pausing at its base and then working up to her ear, lapping at the erogenous zone just beneath it until she squirmed against plastic made slick from her body heat. He didn't say a word, nor did he issue a single command. Not that he could if he'd wanted to because his mouth was fully occupied with working its way down her body. He'd reached her breasts and sucked a solid nipple into his mouth, holding it there with his teeth. It was the first harsh thing he'd done, and she felt her reaction more fiercely because it was so unexpected.

Finally, one of his hands came into play. He moulded that breast as he continued to feast on the nipple, sinking his fingers into her firm flesh again and again, almost as though he couldn't quite believe what he'd set in motion. Porcha couldn't believe it either. Troy was the best endowed of the three, but there really wasn't much in it. Besides, it wasn't what a guy had but how he deployed it that made the difference. Troy liked it hard, Beck liked to punish, but Adam enjoyed making her crazy. He managed it this morning without even using his hands and was doing it again now. Thick blond curls fell over her breasts as he bent his head and continued to suckle, bringing Porcha close to orgasm. Again.

Damn it, he'd noticed the way she'd started to squirm and immediately pulled back, tapping her pussy lightly with the flat of his hand.

"Not yet," he said quietly. "We have to have dessert first."

"Dessert?" Porcha shook her head. This was no time to think about food.

"I'm the gourmet of the group, don't forget." His lips hovered inches above hers, and he spoke so quietly that she barely heard him. "I like to eat in all sorts of different ways, depending on the appetite that most urgently needs satisfying."

"And what appetite would that be, master?"

"You'll see."

He reached across to the floor and picked up a bowl, scooped a finger inside, and held it against her lips. Instinctively, she lapped. It was thick, sugary double cream. How did he know that she loved cream? He didn't, but she figured it had to be a safe bet. Everyone liked cream, didn't they?

"Gorgeous," she said, running her tongue over her lips to make sure she hadn't left any behind.

"Try this."

Adam dipped a finger in another bowl and held it out to her. Rich, dark chocolate sauce.

"Delicious."

"My own recipe."

"To what use do you put your own recipes in the bedroom, master?"

"You'll see. Now, keep absolutely still."

Adam used a spatula to carefully spread chocolate sauce all over the peaks of her breasts, rather as though he was frosting a cake. When he was satisfied with his handiwork, he finished off with generous dollops of cream.

"Christ!" she heard Beck say.

"I'm starving."

Adam dropped his head to her tits and used his teeth as well as his lips to scoop up every last scrap of the confection. Porcha, her hands out of play, made do with lifting her body closer to his mouth, desperate for him to consume more of her breasts. She spread her legs wide, hoping to entice him lower, but he remained crouched on one side of her, diligently working on her aching tits.

"That's made me thirsty."

He reached for a bottle of chilled wine and poured a little in her belly button. She giggled as the cold liquid ran off her body. Adam's tongue was there before it could reach the sheet, lapping at her as much as at the wine, tickling as it rasped against her skin. She could no longer see what he was doing but felt more chocolate and cream being drizzled over her body as Adam slowly licked his way toward her cunt. God, if he didn't get there soon she'd die!

As though sensing her urgency, his weight left the bed altogether. An outraged groan escaped her lips, and she wondered if he'd punish her for it. Before she had time to decide, he rejoined her and straddled her body, his heavy balls dangling close to her chin.

"Your turn to eat."

He guided an erect cock covered with confection close to her lips. Porcha lapped delicately at its tip, teasing him in the same way that he had her. Unlike her, Adam seemed to be able to stand the torture. She should have known that would be the case. All three of them had ten times more discipline than she ever would. It must be a military thing.

Chocolate melted and dripped from his prick all over her chest.

"You need to take it all in if you don't wanna finish up too sticky," Adam told her, a smile in his voice.

Yeah, she kind of got that bit and sucked him deep into the back of her throat. She'd barely done so before he pulled himself free and abruptly left her again. *What now?* She wasn't left in ignorance for long. His hands rubbed chocolate and cream into her pubis and then deep inside her.

"Oh!"

"Feels good, right?"

"Right."

Adam's blond head hovered above hers as he took his weight on his arms. "You have no idea how erotic you look all covered in chocolate and cream."

"We have," Beck said, panting.

"I'm tempted to lick it off, but I might just fuck it in a bit deeper first. Would you like that, Porcha?"

"Yes, God yes!"

"Then ask me nicely."

"Please, Adam. I need to be fucked."

"But Troy just fucked you." Adam quirked a taunting brow. "Are you saying he didn't do a good enough job?"

"He was masterful, but I want you as well."

"She *is* greedy, isn't she," he said, presumably to Troy and Beck.

"Needs a good spanking, if you ask me," Beck responded.

"No one did." Adam dangled his prick tantalizingly close to her pussy. "Sure you want this, sugar?"

"No, I've changed my mind."

Troy and Beck roared with laughter.

"Better do it anyway," Troy suggested. "Before all that chocolate melts."

Adam growled and drove himself into her. Porcha cried out with pleasure as he sank all the way home and the cream squelched out of her with a loud sucking sound. She lifted her legs and wrapped them round him without being told to. She needed him as deep as she could get him. Their bodies adhered together with sticky chocolate as they moved in unison, pleasure spangling as Adam's lips covered hers in a kiss made sweet with a combination of passion and cocoa.

"That's it, baby," he said, breaking the kiss. "Move with me. Take it all. Let me get good and deep."

"Adam, I need to come. Say it's okay."

"It's okay. Come for me, darlin'. Let it go. Let me hear you scream."

Porcha didn't need telling twice. Sensation reverberated through her like thunder as Adam drove himself into her, stirring her passion until there was nowhere for it to go and it was released in a spine-tingling orgasm. She bellowed his name to the rafters as she clamped his cock tight inside her vagina, milking it until she was slick with sweat and every nerve ending in her body sang its pleasure.

"Jesus, Porcha, what are you doing to me?"

She was still in the throes of her orgasm when Adam lost control and spurted deep inside her. A second orgasm hit her before the first had faded. She closed her eyes as it consumed her and simply hung on for the ride.

Adam and Porcha lay side by side, slick, sticky, and totally spent. She felt the bed dip as Troy and Beck joined her.

"Any of that cream left?" Troy asked.

"Plenty."

"Then let's have some fun."

Adam rubbed chocolate and cream into one breast, Beck dealt with the other, and Troy did the same with her midriff, working his way toward her cunt.

"Much as I'd like to make her wait," Troy said, "I think this cream's gonna melt."

"Right."

"Her ass is mine," Beck said, moving into position.

"I'll take the front door," Troy said.

"Guess I know where I am then," Adam said, winking at Porcha as he moved into position.

Porcha climaxed three times before any of them came. She simply didn't care if she was way out of control. Surely that was the point of having three hunks fucking her at the same time? She took everything on offer, always wanting more. They were all slick with confection, moving about all over the slippery sheet, the only restriction to their movements being Porcha's restrained arms.

"Fuck it!" Beck screamed. "I gotta let go."

Porcha pushed back as she felt him spurting into her, only to discover that Troy was doing the same thing in her pussy. She moved her hips between them, giving them as much help as she could, whilst gripped by yet another orgasm of her own. How many times could one woman come in the course of an evening?

"Drink it, babe. It's for you."

She sucked on Adam's shaft as he shot into her mouth, feeling him pulsating for what seemed like ages. His cum tasted of chocolate, cream, and what she guessed must be her own juices. The combination trickled down her throat, sweeter than vintage wine.

"Wow!"

Beck and Troy collapsed on either side of her. Adam lay longways across the top of her head, massaging her crown with gentle sweeps of his large hands.

It was a while before any of them had the strength to move. When they eventually did, someone released her hands, someone else kissed her with deep appreciation, and the third went to run the bath.

They took turns in soaping her clean, even washing the confectionary out of her hair. She wasn't surprised when the bath turned into another round of fucking. Beck took her first from behind whilst she leant on Troy's knee for support. Adam took his place the moment Beck slipped out of her. Then it was Troy's turn again. He sat on the steps to the bath with her on his lap, forbidding her to move a muscle whilst he thrust into her from below.

When they were finally all spent, Troy wrapped her in a fluffy towel that swamped her and carried her naked down the stairs, the other two following behind. When they reached her room, Adam pulled the covers back while Troy divested her of the towel and laid her down. Then he climbed in with her. Her body jerked when she realized he planned to spend the night with her. She wondered if one of the others would, too—the bed was easily big enough for three of them—but Adam and Beck merely bent to kiss her goodnight and left the room. Neither of them questioned Troy's arbitrary decision to remain with her. She figured that tomorrow night she'd have a different bedfellow since they appeared to be able to share without any signs of jealousy.

"Go to sleep," Troy said, pulling her into his arms and resting her head on his chest. "You must be exhausted."

She opened her eyes very wide. "You want to sleep?"

"We'll have some fun when we wake up, if you ask me nicely, but right now you need to get some rest." He dropped a light kiss on her lips. "Busy day tomorrow."

"I don't want to think about tomorrow." She smiled up at him. "Tell me about you. Adam says you're from Argentina."

"I was born there, but it's a while since I've been back."

"Why?"

"There's nothing there for me now. Not that there ever really was."

"What, no family?"

"No. I never knew my father, and my mother died when I was twelve. I was the youngest, and my older brothers and sisters all have their own families now."

"And you don't keep in touch?"

"My oldest brother's in prison and likely to stay there for the rest of his life."

"What did he do?"

"Got involved with a vicious gang. Thought he could do as he liked 'cause the rules didn't apply to him. The usual. My sisters are both married to losers and both have a bunch of kids who'll just grow up to repeat the pattern."

"Sounds like you do keep in touch. You seem to know all about them."

"I hear from them occasionally. Usually when they want something." Porcha could hear the contempt in his voice. "No, make that only when they want something, which is usually a handout."

"So you decided to break the mould and go your own way."

Troy shrugged. "Pretty much. I suppose I can't blame them for turning out the way they have. It takes courage to be different. The kids grow up quick in the area I came from…Well, they do if they wanna survive, and my siblings were busy doing just that—blending in and not making waves—so they didn't have a lot of time for me. I didn't like what I saw them getting into, so I got a job doing all the dirty labor for a polo team because I liked horses, had a way with them, and came cheap."

"I can just imagine you on horseback. You'd be worth looking at."

Troy dropped a kiss on her forehead. "You like horses?"

"Yes, I used to ride a million years ago, back in England."

"Well, my team came to the States for a series of matches when I was fifteen. I decided that I liked it here. There were more opportunities for a guy prepared to get his hands dirty, so I stayed."

Porcha smiled. "Just like that?"

He tweaked her nose. "Just like that. It's not so hard if you're not too particular who you do business with. I eventually managed to get fake papers—you don't want to know how—and finished up in the military." He expelled a long breath. "That's about all there is to know about me, baby. My life's an open book apart from that."

She snorted. "Hardly. I think you have a lot of secrets inside that head of yours, but I also think that's precisely where they'll stay, no matter what I say."

"Wouldn't be much good at what I do if I couldn't keep a secret." He pulled her more tightly against his chest. "Now go to sleep, darling. Like I said, we have a lot to do tomorrow."

"Good night, Troy," she said sleepily.

"Night, babe."

Chapter Fourteen

"I can't sleep if you're looking at me."

"How do you know I'm looking? You've got your eyes closed."

"Aren't you?"

"Just admiring the view. Now stop stalling and get some rest."

In spite of her protestations, she fell asleep almost immediately, totally exhausted. That was hardly surprising, given the things they'd had her do that night. Her breathing was light and even, barely disturbing the hairs on Troy's chest. He watched her, feelings of fierce protectiveness assailing him from all sides. She was astonishing. The way she'd embraced their games with such wholehearted enthusiasm had gotten to him, and there was no way in the world he'd let her go when this was all over. He had a feeling the others felt the same way. He'd talk to them about it, once her business was settled, and work something out.

His mind drifted to their schedule for the following day. If things went to plan and Woollard showed up, they'd capture him, find out what the hell was going on, who was after Porcha, and why. He went over and over the details, meticulous and single-minded as always, and couldn't think of anything they'd overlooked. So why was he feeling so edgy about the whole damned escapade? Was there something he'd overlooked? He sure as hell didn't think so, but there were so many imponderables about this whole damned business that he couldn't shake the feeling of unease.

Troy eventually dozed, his dreams interspersed with images of Porcha chained to his strappado as he fucked her beautiful ass. But

Woollard's face kept intruding, taunting him. He was yelling that Troy would never keep Porcha, she was his. *What the fuck?*

"Troy!"

A hand shook his shoulder and he reacted instinctively, grabbing that hand and rolling over the body that it belonged to. Only when he felt Porcha's soft curves gelling with the hard planes of his own body did he realize what he'd done. He wasn't supporting his weight and immediately rolled off her before he flattened her.

"Sorry, babe."

"You were shouting in your sleep," she said, brushing a hand across his forehead. "Are you all right?"

"Sure. Sorry about that. What time is it?"

She glanced at the clock. "Six thirty."

"Time I was up."

"You already are." She giggled as she flicked a finger against his erection.

He chuckled. "A permanent condition when I'm anywhere near you."

"Hmm, I see your problem." She nibbled the end of her index finger. "What can we do about that, then?"

"What indeed."

Troy lowered his head and kissed the little vixen. He was never going to do anything else, right from the moment she woke him from his dream and his cock sat up and paid close attention to proceedings. It was completely beyond him to resist her lush body, the temptation of that sweet pussy, those gorgeous tits, her endless legs. He deepened the kiss, rolled on his back, and pulled her on top of him. She leaned into the kiss, her tits brushing against his chest as she sucked his lower lip between her teeth and nibbled at it. His hands reached for her breasts, dangling tantalizingly just beyond his grasp. He was unsurprised to discover that her nipples were rock hard, and he pinched them between his thumbs and forefingers, well aware that she wouldn't want him to treat her gently. Just as well, because Troy seldom did gentle.

Still kissing her, he placed his hands on her waist and lifted her. She got the message and positioned herself over his cock, wriggling with impatience to take it all.

"Ride it, babe," he said, breaking the kiss and smiling up at her.

"If you insist."

She sank down on him, closing her eyes as he slid into her and his hands reclaimed her tits. They settled into a slow, easy rhythm, letting the feelings grow in their own time. She was so goddamned sexy, even though her features were still puffy with sleep. Tangled hair fell across her face as she rode him, her remarkable eyes sparkling with life and anticipation even though she'd only just opened them. Troy groaned as the full weight of her breasts settled heavily in his hands each time she lowered herself on him. He increased the tempo, for once having no desire to make her wait.

"I want you to tie me up," she said. "I love it when I'm at your complete mercy."

"Not this morning, babe. Wrong time and place. Right now we're just gonna fuck ourselves awake." He pinched her nipples hard enough to make her squeal. "But tonight we'll play a few new games. We'll keep you bound and gagged all night, make you do all sorts of crazy things, thrash your ass and your cunt 'cause you like having your pussy slapped, don't you?" She swallowed hard and nodded. "I have a lot more toys yet that you haven't tried, and we'll catch it all on film. Would you like that?"

She sank down hard and groaned. "You know I would. Do you have cameras up there?"

"We've got enough cameras in this house to make Steven Spielberg weep with envy."

She groaned as he drove a little deeper into her. "Why?"

"Because we're cautious bastards who've pissed a lot of people off in our time. We don't want our personal space invaded by the bad guys."

"Oh."

Porcha rotated her shoulders, sending her hair cascading down her back as she tilted her head back and closed the eyes, sensation clearly overwhelming her. "I need you, Troy. Make me come, please!"

Her anguished cry did it for Troy. Besides, he had preparations to make and no time to linger. He thrust his pelvis upward, and she met him perfectly, thrashing down at precisely the same moment so that he was as deep inside her as he could possibly get. The door opened just as they both climaxed, and Adam stood there, grinning as he watched their performance.

"All the headboard banging woke me up," he said when Porcha collapsed, spent, on top of him.

Troy laughed as he extracted himself from beneath her. He knew what Adam really wanted.

"All yours, buddy," he said, placing a kiss on the tip of her nose, climbing from the bed, and heading for his own shower.

"All ours, you mean," a naked Beck said as he passed him in the passageway and headed for Porcha's room as well.

Troy hadn't been downstairs for long when the other two guys joined him. He'd known they'd be quick. When it came to their work they were all pretty focused. Adam poured coffee for him and Beck and joined Troy at the table. He was checking his weapons.

"You anticipating problems?" Beck asked.

Troy shot his buddy a look that said *don't be so naïve.* "I always anticipate problems. That's what keeps us alive."

"Do you think he'll come?" Adam asked, assembling the ingredients for a massive fry up. None of them liked to work on an empty stomach.

"If he intercepts that e-mail then I don't see how he can afford not to. He wants Porcha badly enough to take risks."

Beck nodded. "I can relate to that."

"I think we all can," Troy responded with a heavy sigh.

"What is it, Troy?" Adam asked, turning away from the hob where he had a pan full of bacon sizzling away. "Is there something you're not telling us?"

"No, nothing." He shook his head. "It just doesn't feel right, that's all."

"It can hardly be a trap because we set the thing up," Beck pointed out.

"I know that, but I keep thinking we've overlooked something."

"You're just anxious because it's Porcha," Adam said. "We all are. We don't usually get emotionally involved with our assignments."

"Yeah, that's kinda what I figured but—"

"The three of us can cover that mall," Beck said reassuringly, "and Porcha will be safe here. No one can get past our security, not in broad daylight—"

Adam flinched. "Unless they shoot their way in."

"They'd need to know she was here," Beck pointed out, "and no one does."

"You're right," Troy said, still uneasy.

"Leave one of us here with her if you're that worried."

"Nah, it'll take all three of us to cover the mall." Troy shook his head. "It'll be all right, I guess."

"You never guess," Beck said, clearly picking up on his anxiety.

Adam plonked plates of food in front of them, and they got into it, all conversation briefly halted. The only disturbance was the scrape of silverware against plates and the steady voice of the newscaster pouring from the television fixed to the wall behind the table.

"All fucking bad news as always," Beck complained.

"Wouldn't be newsworthy otherwise," Adam said, helping himself to a second slice of toast.

They'd cleared away and were all checking their weapons when Porcha drifted in, looking as fresh and lovely as though she'd slept twelve hours solid rather than spent most of the night being fucked by one or all of them. She wore jeans and a sleeveless top *and* had put a bra on.

"Morning again, gorgeous," Beck said, pecking her cheek.

But even he was distracted. Nothing, not even the lovely Porcha, came between the three of them when they were preparing for an assignment.

"There's coffee made," Adam said. "And I could cook you something."

"I'm quite capable of feeding myself, but thanks for the offer."

"Eat something," Troy said in a tone that brooked no argument. "Even if it's just fruit."

"It's not me that's going anywhere."

"No, but you never know what the day might bring."

Porcha kissed his cheek and obediently reached for a piece of fruit.

* * * *

Porcha watched her three guys in business mode, secreting an astonishing number of guns and knives about their persons, communicating in a kind of shorthand she didn't understand and which she was excluded from anyway. Seeing such a tight unit preparing to go in to bat for her ought to have filled her with confidence. It did, but she also feared that one or all of them could be injured in their fight to keep her safe. Woollard was no pussycat and would almost certainly turn up mob handed. The thought of any of them getting hurt because of her almost crucified her. She wouldn't be able to bear the guilt if any of them came back with so much as a scratch.

They looked focused yet calm in their cargo pants and sleeveless vests—attire that made them look like millions of others guys on a Florida weekday morning. The only difference was the miniarsenal of weapons, and perhaps the combat boots that were a bit hot and heavy for the climate.

Her eyes burned into one handsome profile after the other, loving them all, grateful to them for wanting to help her when they didn't need to, especially after they'd had everything they could possibly want from her. Weren't men supposed to go cool when they'd got their collective ends away?

"Okay, babe," Troy said. "You know what to do while we're gone." She nodded, but he spelt it out anyway. "Keep all the doors locked. If anyone knocks, don't answer, and if you have any concerns at all, ring one of us straight away."

"Our phones will probably be on vibrate," Adam said. "We can't afford to have them going off if we're trying to keep out of sight, but we'll check them regularly."

They all turned toward the television when the talking head, a little breathlessly, announced breaking news.

We've just heard that the body of Miami business man Salvador Gonzalez has been found in a Mexican back street. He had been beaten and shot.

All three guys reached out to touch Porcha. The news flashed pictures of a dirty back street in Mexico, "experts" pontificated, hinting at his connection to the drug cartels, but Porcha barely heard the words.

"Well, now it's official," she said, wondering why she didn't feel anything at all. Sal had robbed her of the essence that made her the person she was, but he'd still been her husband, and she'd loved him once. In some respects, she always would.

"Says so on the news, so it must be true," Beck said, but there was sympathy rather than flippancy in his tone.

"The king is dead, long live the king," muttered Adam.

Porcha fixed him with a gaze. "What do you mean?"

"If this was about Woollard wanting to take over Sal's drugs business," Troy said, "he had to let the world, or more specifically, Sal's rivals, know that he was in control."

"I'm surprised he waited so long for Sal's body to be *discovered*," Beck said. "I would imagine the sharks are already circling."

"You gonna be all right, babe?" Troy asked, slipping an arm round her shoulders. "Want one of us to stay with you?"

"No." She expelled a deep sigh. "I'll be fine. You guys go and finish this thing."

"Keep that little gun of yours close by, just in case," Beck added. "Not that we anticipate any trouble this end, but it's best to be prepared."

"Do you need to go already?" Porcha had never been a needy person, but she had a bad feeling about this and was suddenly afraid to let them go. "There's over an hour yet before I'm supposed to be at that mall."

"We need to set ourselves up there," Troy said. "If Woollard thinks you're gonna be there, he'll be early as well."

"Oh, I see." She wrapped her arms round Troy's neck and kissed his lips, repeating the process with the other two. "Stay safe, all of you," she said censoriously. "And get back here as soon as you can."

"Count on it," Adam said.

"Whilst you're gone, I shall amuse myself by dreaming up a few games that I might like to try out on you all later." She fluttered her lashes at them in a deliberate effort to lighten the mood. "Am I allowed to make suggestions or will that get me punished?"

The guys were laughing as they headed for the door that led to the stairway to the garage.

"Lock the door and shoot the bolts after us," Troy said. "We'll honk the horn when we come back so you know it's us and can let us back in."

"Who else would it be?"

"That's what worries me," she thought she heard Troy mutter.

Porcha listened to their truck roar into life, heard the garage door open and close, and locked herself in upstairs as instructed. She slipped her little gun into the back of her jeans and wondered what she was supposed to do with herself now. The house seemed very large and very empty without the guys. She wandered into the kitchen, but there was nothing for her to do there. They were meticulously neat and tidy and never ate without clearing up immediately afterwards. Military discipline, she supposed.

She gravitated toward the living room, stared out at the water, but couldn't settle. In the study—Troy's territory—she glanced at all the various screens, with no idea what half of them were for. She ran her finger down the spines of hundreds of books, all well read. But reading was out of the question, as was watching television. The discovery of Sal's body was everywhere, and she didn't want to hear what they were saying about him.

Too on edge to settle to anything, Porcha continued her restless prowl round the house with no idea what she was looking for. She invaded each of their bedrooms in turn, able to identify which room belonged to whom because each guy expressed his personality in the few possessions he kept in his space. Apart from obsessive neatness, the one thing that all had in common was that they didn't carry any emotional baggage. No pictures of wives, girlfriends, parents, siblings. No old letters, greetings cards, or sentimental knickknacks. It was as though they were ready to take off and not come back at any given time.

That knowledge depressed Porcha and also told her all she needed to know about her relationship with the guys. She was a temporary distraction, nothing more than that, and once Woollard was taken care of, she'd be expected to move on.

"Get real, Porcha," she said aloud. "You've always known that. Make the most of it whilst it lasts and then let them go without making a fuss."

Back in the living room again, she slumped in a chair and flicked through a magazine with no idea as to its subject matter. It could have been *Mercenaries' Weekly* for all she knew, or cared. It probably was. She glanced at her watch for what had to be the thousandth time since they'd left, and sighed. They *had* to have been gone for more than two hours, surely?

The phone rang, sounding unnaturally loud in the otherwise-quiet house, making her start violently. They hadn't said anything about not answering the phone. Besides, it could be them checking on her. She grabbed the receiver.

"Hello."

"Is that Ms. Ballantine?"

Porcha's heart rate increased at the sound of the unfamiliar female voice. Phone calls from strangers almost always spelt trouble. "Who wants to know?"

"This is Tampa General Hospital, ICU."

Hospital? "Yes," she said cautiously.

"This is Ms. Ballantine?"

"Yes, it is." And how the hell did a hospital know where to find her? "What can I do for you?"

"We have a Mr. Ganelli here—"

Porcha gasped. "Georgio?"

"Yes, he's had a heart attack, I'm afraid. We didn't know who to call, but he kept saying your name, and we found your number in his pocketbook."

"How bad is he?"

"He's stable but mostly unconscious, and I'm afraid the prognosis isn't good." The nurse paused when Porcha didn't speak. "We thought you might like to know."

"I'll be right there."

Porcha hung up, frantic with worry. Her first thought was how to get to the hospital. There were two flashy cars in the garage that Beck lavished tender loving care on, and she knew how to open the garage door. The guys wouldn't be happy, but she'd ring them and leave a message so they'd know where to find her.

"Slow down, Porcha, and think this through," she said aloud. "There's no rush. Georgio isn't going anywhere. Why does this feel so contrived?"

Common sense kicked in as soon as her panic subsided. Even if Georgio *did* have her name in his pocketbook, which, given how cautious he was, was extremely unlikely, he wouldn't have had this telephone number as well. Her heart thumped against her rib cage. Someone knew where she was and was trying to get her to leave the house. Panic trickled down her spine.

How? How had they found her?

She picked up the phone again and dialed Troy. It went straight to message divert. *Damn!* She left a brief account of what had happened. Then she went into the study and picked up the secure line Troy had used to call Georgio, dialing his number from memory. Something told her Georgio was alive and well and giving his staff merry hell in his downtown Tampa offices. She sure as hell hoped so, anyway.

Before she could place the call, a miniexplosion rocked the building and the front door flew in. Porcha froze for a moment. Hell, what to do? She glanced round the living room, all out of options. If she went into the yard she'd finish up backed against the water. Porcha was petrified of water and couldn't take that chance. If she went upstairs they'd simply follow her up there. There was only one thing for it. She'd just have to fight it out.

Feeling icily calm, Porcha ran into the study, crouched behind the desk and aimed her gun at the four armed men who charged up the stairs.

Chapter Fifteen

"He ain't coming," Adam said into the wrist microphone that, Secret Service–like, kept him in communication with the others.

"I think you're right," Troy agreed.

They'd been here for almost an hour now watching ordinary people going about their business. The time for Porcha's rendezvous had been twenty minutes ago, and no one was lying in wait for her. They knew that for a fact. One or all of them had eyeballed every person and vehicle that had entered the small strip mall in the last hour, and nothing had triggered their suspicions. They'd visited all the business premises, too, both front and back, and found nothing untoward.

"There's a woman with no mirrors in her house at four o'clock," Beck said.

Troy chuckled as he saw an overweight woman wearing a skirt that revealed way too much thigh waddling in his direction. Leave it to Beck to liven up a dreary stakeout.

"Let's give it another quarter of an hour and then meet back at the truck," Troy said.

He pulled his phone from his pocket and checked his messages, keeping half an eye on the mall, convinced now that they were wasting their time. His heart rate increased when he saw one missed call from his home number. He listened to Porcha's message, black ice trickling through his veins when he heard what she had to say. Why the hell hadn't he taken the call? It wasn't like he'd exactly had his hands full when he felt it vibrate in his pocket.

Panic was briefly replaced by relief when she said Georgio's illness had to be a hoax and she didn't plan to leave the house. She was pretty damned smart. Most women would have hit the ground running and asked questions only when it was too late. Then Troy realized what the message actually meant, and panic came crashing in on him again with twice its previous velocity.

Someone knew where she was.

"Back to the truck now!"

Troy yelled the order to the others, running in that direction and hitting the button on his phone that would connect him with home. It rang and rang without being answered, which is when he knew why he'd felt so uneasy about this entire setup. They'd been second-guessed the whole way, and as soon as they were out of the house, Woollard had moved in on Porcha. Or bloody soon would. If she didn't dash out in response to the bogus hospital call, they'd find a way to get in. Their home was a fortress, and the average person would never get past first base if they tried to break in. Woollard, as Sal Gonzalez's right-hand man, had to be anything but average.

Adam and Beck joined him at a run, not the slightest bit out of breath. All that training paid off when it counted most. Beck took one look at Troy's face, slid behind the wheel of the truck, and gunned the motor.

"What's happened?" Adam asked.

Troy filled them in.

"Shit!" Beck floored the accelerator. "We need to get to her before anyone else does."

"When I get my hands on Woollard, he's a fucking dead man," Adam said.

"You'll be right in line behind me." Troy's jaw ached as he ground his teeth with impotent rage.

Beck did a smooth overtaking maneuver to get past an old lady hogging the middle of the road and took the next left exit on two wheels. It was at times like this that Beck's pride and joy, his Dodge truck, came into its own. He'd spent hours tinkering with it, and it could now outrun just about anything else, especially with Beck behind the wheel.

Never had its qualities been in greater need.

"What's the holdup?" Troy asked Beck, who was already doing twice the speed limit.

Beck slammed his foot down a little harder.

"I can't believe we fucked this up so comprehensively," Adam fumed.

Unfortunately, Troy could.

* * * *

Porcha knew there were four of them. She could see their feet from beneath the desk, could hear them talking in Spanish, making no attempt to keep quiet. Well, why would they after they'd made such a racket getting in here? They knew she was alone and didn't feel threatened, which was their first mistake. Porcha, far from being afraid, felt deadly calm. She even found time to wonder why Woollard had sent Mexicans to do his dirty work. She'd thought he'd come himself for this one. Perhaps he'd gone to make sure the guys got held up. Whatever. She probably wouldn't be able to fight all four of these thugs, but she'd sure as hell get one or two of them before they got her. They probably had orders to take her alive, whereas she had no compunction about lessening their joint life expectancy.

What to do? They were tearing through the living quarters, throwing things aside, breaking things, turning furniture over, simply because they could. It was only a matter of time before they found her in here. There was no place to run, and she had an urgent desire to protect the guys' rooms. She absolutely didn't want them ransacked. She didn't want them polluting the playroom, either.

As one of them stuck his head round the office door, she stood up and smiled at him, keeping her gun out of sight.

"Looking for me?" she asked.

He blinked in surprise, and then a slow, satisfied smile spread across his face as his gaze travelled the length of her body.

"Found her," he shouted to the others. "Come on then, love," he said. "The boss wants a word with you."

"Certainly."

She offered him her sweetest, most innocent smile. He responded with a smile of his own, just like men always did when she smiled at them. He'd lowered his gun, still grinning and smacking his lips. His expression was almost comical when she raised her own weapon and he realized what she intended to do. Before he had a chance to do anything to defend himself, she placed two neat shots clean through the centre of his heart.

He crumpled to the floor with a look of abject shock on his face, just as his buddies crowded round her. Before she could get any more shots off, one of them knocked the gun from her hand and twisted her arm up her back. *Big mistake, buster!* She slumped against him, waiting for him to loosen his grip and relax his guard. The moment he did so, she used the same technique she'd practised on Beck, utilizing his own body weight to throw him over her shoulder.

He landed on the desk so heavily that the wood cracked, as did the man's arm. He cried out, swearing prolifically in Spanish. Porcha wished she'd dumped him down harder, at the same time glad that Troy's precious monitors merely wobbled on the broken desk but didn't slide off it. Why that should matter at a time when she was fighting, at the very least for her freedom, she couldn't have said, but such was the disjointed nature of the thoughts that spiralled through her mind.

By now, the two other guys were taking her more seriously. She, a helpless female, had killed one man and injured another. That wouldn't go down well with Woollard. He hated sloppy workmanship.

"Come on, love," said the guy who was obviously their leader. "We have orders not to kill you, but no one said anything about not hurting you."

Porcha was beaten. Any slim hope that the guys might have picked up her message faded as she reluctantly moved toward them. It was either that or have them forcibly remove her, and the thought of them pawing her made her skin crawl. As she forced her feet forward, the phone rang. She automatically reached for it, but the boss man placed his hand over it before she could pick it up.

"I don't think so."

Porcha shrugged. "I guess they'll have to call back," she said, her attitude so matter-of-fact that she could see her captors didn't quite know what to make of her.

The guy with the broken arm struggled to his feet, holding his useless limb beneath the elbow, howling and grousing, his eyes shooting daggers at Porcha.

"What shall we do about him?" one of them asked, pointing to the dead man.

"Let's leave him for her friends to dispose of." The boss spat on their dead colleague. "Stupid fuck shouldn't have flirted with the girl. He got what he deserved."

Thoughts of being at Woollard's mercy resurrected Porcha's fighting spirit. After the joy of being with her trio of lovers, she absolutely would not submit to a prig like Woollard. Whilst the one of the remaining able-bodied guys helped his injured buddy, Porcha assessed her options. The boss grasped Porcha's arm firmly, and she allowed herself to be dragged toward the front door. Her opportunity came when the boss eased his grip on her whilst he checked to see if the coast was clear. The other guy had to hold his buddy up since he was in some distress. Big men did cry, it seemed. She vaguely wondered where Woollard had found them. They didn't look familiar. Must have come back from Mexico with him, she supposed.

As soon as the grip on her arm was released completely, Porcha spun in a circle, hoping to catch the boss's throat in a scissor action between her legs. Unfortunately, the space was too confined, and she had to make do with bringing her knee up into his groin. It was her final chance to break free, and she put all her pent-up anger behind the move. Boss man howled, a combination of surprise and pain, instinctively doubling over to protect his now-damaged goods.

"Get her!" he yelled at the other guy when she took off at a sprint.

She got fifty yards down the road before the other guy grabbed her legs and brought her crashing down on the blacktop. Her world spun, and her arms, which had taken the brunt of the fall, burned where she badly scraped them.

"That's it, you damned meddling bitch!"

She kicked out and caught him in the midriff. She heard the air leave his lungs as he swore at her.

"Nice try, bitch, but I ain't no pushover." The guy pulled her to her feet and slapped her face hard. "Quit fighting. You're coming with us."

Porcha was very much afraid that this time he might well be right, because she had no fight left in her.

* * * *

Beck screeched to a halt outside their house. Troy was out of the truck before it even stopped and growled when he saw their broken front door swinging open and all that it implied.

"We're too late," Adam said, stating the obvious.

Troy dashed inside, closely followed by the others. They each took the stairs three at a time, barely noticing the mess in their living room, but the sight of a man bleeding out on the study floor, not to mention the broken desk, did get their attention. Troy felt for a pulse and found none.

"Mexican?" Beck asked.

"Looks that way."

Troy felt in the dead man's pockets and found a photo of the three of them standing on Porcha's doorstep in Tampa. They'd been photographed, obviously by the watcher, when Troy took his shades off so Porcha could identify him. A long-lensed camera had got a perfect shot of his profile.

"Now we know how they found us," he said, grinding his teeth. "We obviously looked as though we'd been sent to protect Porcha. They only had to show this around people in the know, throw a bit of cash at the problem, and someone would have identified us sooner or later. We're quite well known."

"Figures," Beck said bitterly. "Loyalty ain't what it used to be."

"And a lot of people have waited a long time to get one over on us," Troy reminded them.

"How we gonna get Porcha back?" Adam asked.

Beck kicked the dead man with the toe of his boot. "And who killed this guy?"

"Let's find out."

Troy pressed a button that controlled the camera in the study. The only sound as they waited for it to whirl back to the time of Porcha's call to Troy was their heavy breathing. The screen flickered into life at the appropriate place, showing a completely empty study. Then Porcha flew into the room, gun in hand, and hid behind the desk.

Adam shook his head. "Stupid place to hide."

"She should have stood above the stairs and shot the bastards through the open slats as they came up," Troy said.

"She must have been terrified," Beck pointed out. "No time to think straight."

There were grim grunts of satisfaction when the dead guy walked into the room and Porcha stood up and popped him.

"Atagirl!" Beck punched the air.

In spite of the grim realization that Porcha had been stolen from beneath their noses, all three guys briefly smiled when they saw her throw the guy over the desk. They watched until she was led away, and Troy switched off. He took a picture of the dead man on his cell and sent it to Georgio. He then pressed the button on the speakerphone and rang him, filling him in on the events. None of them wasted time on voicing regrets. They were too focused and professional for that, although right then Troy was questioning their right to call themselves professionals. They'd been led by the balls on this one, start to finish. He should have gone with his instincts and not let Porcha out of his sight.

This was all his fault. He'd acted on assumptions and hadn't bothered to check his facts, simply because he was emotionally involved, desperate to keep Porcha safe. He thumped his thigh with considerable force. He was every sort of arrogant idiot that ever lived, all rolled into one.

"Do you know the guy?" he asked as soon as Georgio got the picture his end.

"No, can't say I've had the pleasure."

"Hang on, Adam's downloading a picture of their leader from the video feed here."

As soon as the picture went through, Georgio inhaled sharply. "Ah, shit!"

"That bad?" Troy asked, hitching one buttock cautiously on the edge of his broken desk.

"Worse. He's head honcho for one of Sal's main rivals in the drugs business. Does the name Sanchez-Punto mean anything to you?"

"So they're not working for Woollard?"

"Doesn't look that way. This isn't good, Troy."

Troy exhaled sharply. "Tell me something I don't know."

"You heard on the news that Sal's body's been found?"

"Yeah, we heard. They'll be a lot of jockeying for position now."

"Why would Sanchez-Punto want Porcha?" Adam asked.

"Perhaps he really does think she knows where Sal's diamonds are."

"Any idea where they'd take her?"

"Miami, I should think. That's Sanchez-Punto's patch, and he'd feel more comfortable there. He has a warehouse that he uses for his legitimate business. Of course, if he takes her to a house rather than his place of business then we're fucked."

"See if you can find out what other places he has in Miami while we head on over there," Troy said. "Oh, and can you get someone over here to fix our front door, get rid of the rubbish, and stay here until the place is secure?"

"I'm on it."

"One other thing, Georgio. Do you have a phone number for Sal's house in Jupiter?"

"Sure." Georgio reeled it off, and Troy programmed it straight into his cell. "Why do you want it?"

"If Woollard isn't behind this and it was Sanchez-Punto who popped Gonzalez, then he might want to help us get his boss's wife back."

"What if he doesn't give a shit about her?" Adam asked. "Porcha hates him, and she thought the feeling was mutual."

"That's a chance we'll just have to take."

"Besides, we need some inside help," Beck added. "We know fuck all about the drugs hierarchy."

"Be careful," Georgio warned. "These guys don't fuck about."

"Nor do we," Troy said in a tone of steely determination as he cut the connection. "Come on," he said to Adam and Beck. "Let's go get her back."

Chapter Sixteen

"This way, madam," the thug said with exaggerated politeness.

Porcha felt blood trickling down her arms as he pulled her to her feet and propelled her in the direction of a Cadillac with blacked-out windows. Every bone in her body hurt like hell, and it felt as though she'd lost half the skin from her forearms. Her face was red raw where the guy had whacked her hard enough to make her teeth rattle, and she was as mad as hell for letting herself get caught.

But at least she was still alive.

The guy pushed her facedown over the hood of the car, pulled her arms behind her back with enough force to make her eyes water, and bound them with duct tape. It was broad daylight. Surely someone, some nosy neighbour, must have seen what was happening and called the police? But there was no sign of life in the street and no twitching drapes that indicated someone alive still felt a sense of civic duty. Not that she would have expected much else. This was a residential area, and it was a normal working day. No one was at home or, if they were, they were minding their own damned business.

Porcha was pushed into the back of the car. Without the use of her hands, she fell awkwardly onto the seat and only just avoided colliding with the person already there. The goon whose arm she'd broken was barely conscious but still muttered a stream of curses in Spanish when he saw her. At least there was a wide armrest between him and her so she didn't need to get too close. Even so, his fetid breath and evil expression made her gut roil. They might have been ordered not to kill her, but she got the feeling that given half a chance this guy would take his revenge any way he could get it. If word of him being outsmarted by a woman did the rounds, as it probably would, his reputation as a hard man would be impaired beyond redemption.

She turned away from him and stared out the window, assessing her situation, wondering what she could do to help herself. There had to be something. The boss was in the passenger seat, and the only remaining able-bodied goon was concentrating on driving. That made it one against one. Only problem was, she didn't have a weapon, nor did she have the use of her hands.

"In case you're wondering, Mrs. Gonzalez," the boss man said conversationally, "we're taking you to Miami to have a little chat with our boss."

"Woollard," she muttered beneath her breath. "I can hardly wait."

"Woollard?" He turned to look at her, genuine surprise in his expression. "Don't imagine that he'll help you."

"But I thought—"

"What did you think?" The guy curled his upper lip. "That you're a beautiful woman, so every man on the planet puts your welfare before his own business?" His cruel laugh echoed round the interior of the car. "You just enjoyed the protection of three tough men, but that didn't do you much good, did it?"

"Where are they?" she asked before she could stop herself. "What have you done to Troy?" she added, almost to herself.

"Troy?"

Damn, he'd heard her. She said Troy's name because she thought of him as their leader, but she cared desperately about them all so shouldn't have displayed weakness by letting on.

"He's someone I employed to help me." She expelled an expansive sigh. "You just can't get the help nowadays but then…" Her gaze flitted over the guy with the broken arm. "You'd know all about that, wouldn't you?"

The guy looked thoroughly pissed off to be reminded about the reduction in his numbers. "If Troy is one of the guys from St. Pete, then I guess they're chasing their tails looking for you. But I wouldn't hold out too much hope if I were you. We're on my turf now, honey."

"Thanks, I'll bear that in mind."

Porcha breathed an inaudible sigh of relief. If the guys had been hurt, this bully wouldn't be able to help boasting about it.

"Forget them. There's nothing they can do for you now. You'd be better off telling the boss what he needs to know."

"Of course," she said sweetly. "He only has to ask. There really was no need for all this strong-arm stuff."

He flashed her a probing look, like he hadn't expected that reaction. "Glad to learn that you've come to your senses. I think you'll find that the days when men were prepared to go that extra mile for you died with your husband. Oh..." His vile smile revealed the yellowing teeth of a heavy smoker. "I almost forgot. My condolences."

Porcha barely heard him. She'd been so intent upon evading capture that only now did it dawn on her that if Woollard wasn't behind the attempts to kidnap her, then someone else had to be. The same someone who'd killed her husband, presumably.

"Does your boss have a name?"

"Mr. Sanchez-Punto is most anxious to make your acquaintance."

She shrugged. "Never heard of him."

"He was one of your husband's main competitors." That self-satisfied grin again. "But not anymore."

"What does he want with me?"

"What do all men want with you?"

"I'm selective."

The guy roared with laughter. "That's not what I heard."

It appeared the conversation was over since the guy turned back and stared at the road ahead. The injured goon next to her seemed to be asleep, and Porcha was grateful for the quiet. It gave her time to think. All that business about her knowing where Sal's diamonds were had to be true. This Sanchez-Punto character was keeping her alive because he thought she had information that he needed. Until she could find a way out of this, or until Troy and the guys came to her rescue, she'd just have to try and perpetuate that myth.

She really didn't have any other choice.

* * * *

Beck was behind the wheel of the truck as they crossed the Sunshine Skyway Bridge and headed for Miami. In the passenger seat, Troy hit the number for Woollard that he'd programmed into his phone, seething with impatience, even though someone at the Jupiter house answered on the first ring.

"I need to talk to Woollard," he said without preamble. "It's about Mrs. Gonzalez."

"Just a moment."

Troy nodded at the guys. "They've gone to get him."

"Just like that?" Adam sounded surprised. "No third degree."

"They're obviously desperate for news of Porcha."

"That's what worries me," Beck said. "I'd almost rather they had her than this Sanchez-Punto character."

"Woollard," came a brisk voice over the line. "Who am I talking to?"

"You want Mrs. Gonzalez back?"

"Of course. You have her?"

"She's been with us for the past couple of days."

"You make it sound as though she no longer is."

"Is this line secure?"

"Yes."

"We believe she's in the hands of Sanchez-Punto."

An angry hiss sounded down the line. "Shit!"

"My feelings exactly."

"Where are you?"

"On our way to Miami. We'll be there this afternoon."

"We need to meet."

"Yes," Troy agreed. "We do."

"Come to the house in Jupiter."

Troy laughed. "Not a chance. We'll meet somewhere neutral."

"You have my word that nothing will happen to you."

"Thanks, but with all due respect, I have no idea what your word's worth."

"Okay, where do you want to meet?"

They agreed on a place on South Beach. There was less chance of an ambush in a crowded place.

"There are three of us," Troy said. "I don't expect to see more than three of you." He paused. "And believe me, we *will* see. We're good at what we do."

"Not that good," Woollard responded acerbically, "or you wouldn't have lost Mrs. Gonzalez."

"Ouch," Troy said, grimacing as he hung up. "I guess I deserved that."

"Do you trust him?" Beck asked.

"Not an inch, but we'll never get into Sanchez-Punto's stronghold without his help. I *do* think we both want to rescue Porcha, even if we have different agendas. Best pool our resources and worry about the fallout afterwards."

"Be careful, Troy," Adam warned. "I don't like the sound of this guy."

"Me neither, but he's a better option that Sanchez-Punto, that's for sure."

"He's our only option," Beck reminded them.

"The way I see it," Troy said after they'd traveled several miles in tense silence, "either Woollard wants Porcha because he doesn't know where the diamonds are either and thinks she does—"

"Or we got it wrong and he's just trying to do the right thing by his boss's widow," Adam finished for him.

"We know from Porcha what he wanted to do to her." Beck thumped the heel of his hand against the steering wheel. "And I'm damned if I'll stand by and let it happen."

"I'm not ecstatic about it myself." Troy expelled a fractured breath. "We'll just have to play it by ear, get a feel for the guy when we meet him, and take it from there. Not that my instincts are serving me too well right now. I was convinced Woollard would show up at that mall today. I stupidly rushed in instead of taking the time to check things out more thoroughly. If I'd done what I usually do, we'd have been there with her today and she'd still be safe."

Adam, seated behind Troy, slapped him on the shoulder. "We let you think you're the boss, but if we hadn't agreed with you we'd have let you know soon enough."

"Yeah, well, we ain't gonna fuck up again."

"Damn right we're not," Adam and Beck said together.

* * * *

"Get out."

It was late afternoon by the time the Cadillac pulled up at a waterside warehouse in a downbeat part of Miami. The fact that the driver backed up his command by openly waving a gun in Porcha's face told her all she hadn't already figured out for herself about the area she was in. The chance of any law-enforcement officials happening along were precisely zero. What few people she did see were minding their own business and certainly wouldn't risk helping her.

She was on her own.

With no other choice available to her, she slid her legs out of the car and struggled awkwardly to her feet with her hands still taped behind her back.

"Inside."

The gun was jabbed painfully in the small of her back. She stumbled toward a side door at the back of the warehouse and stood in front of it. The goon with the gun was obviously as stupid as he looked, because he didn't seem to understand why Porcha didn't open it.

"Oh for fuck's sake!"

The boss reached past her and slammed it open. Porcha tried to memorise everything she saw in the few seconds she had to get her bearings. There was a huge space with tables running its full length and merchandise stacked neatly in boxes down one side of the wall. Some sort of retail supplier, presumably. Since the place was devoid of human presence, it was impossible to see what was in the boxes, so it didn't help her figure out where she was.

"This way."

She was jabbed by the gun again and forced away from the main part of the warehouse, along a short corridor. There were bathrooms on one side and then the door to a room at the back, which she was pushed into. By the looks of things, it was some sort of sickroom.

"Thoughtful of Mr. Sanchez-Punto to have medical facilities on hand in case his employees are taken ill," she said, the strain of pretending to be unconcerned about her situation really starting to tell on her.

"Shut up and get inside."

She was shoved so hard this time that she stumbled and almost fell. The boss caught her arm and saved her at the last moment. The room was about the size of a prison cell—pretty apt, given her current circumstances. There was a hospital-type examination bunk down one wall with a thin pillow and blanket, an uncomfortable-looking upright chair, and a door that led to a toilet. That was it. Absolutely no other furniture or cabinets with locks she could pass the time trying to pick. Perhaps this wasn't a sick bay after all. In which case, Porcha didn't want to think about what other purpose the room might serve.

She took a second look around, just to take her mind off such unpleasant musings. The small window had sturdy-looking bars across it, and there was no other means of escape that she could see.

"Make yourself comfortable, Mrs. Gonzalez," said the goon, leering at her breasts as he cut her hands free.

The boss was standing in the corridor, talking in a deferential tone to someone on the phone. Porcha caught some of what he was saying.

"Yes, sir, she's here now. No, no we definitely weren't followed." He listened. "Well, we were taken by surprise. We lost Pablo, and Luiz has a broken arm. We're taking him to get it fixed right now." He listened some more and then spoke again. "Yes, it was unfortunate. There were several of them that we didn't know about, you see, and they jumped us."

Porcha raised a brow at him and smiled. The boss glowered right back at her, realizing when it was too late that he shouldn't have let her hear his excuses. She'd sure as hell set Sanchez-Punto right when she saw him.

"They got away I'm afraid, sir, but we managed to hold onto the woman. Right, okay then, we'll do that."

"You'll be spending the night here as our guest," he told her, walking fully into the tiny room and making it feel pretty crowded. "Mr. Sanchez-Punto will come and see you first thing in the morning."

"Tell him not to put himself out on my account."

"She's got a real smart mouth on her," the goon said, raising a hand.

"Leave her be!"

"She needs to learn more respect." He dropped his hand with obvious reluctance. "I hate mouthy women."

"Any chance of something to eat?" Porcha asked sweetly. "And some stuff to clean up my injuries." She waved her arms about, giving them an up-close view of the caked blood on her forearms.

"Let her fucking bleed to death," the one she'd heard referred to as Raul grumbled.

"Oh, I'm sure your boss'll be pleased if you let that happen." She rolled her eyes. "Moron!"

"Raul will come back later with something."

Raul's expression told her what he thought of that suggestion, and this time Porcha agreed with him. The last thing she wanted was quality one-on-one time with Raul. Then again, perhaps she did. He was a follower, not a leader. He was also a bully, and he was mad at her. Porcha sat on the edge of the bunk and waved her fingers at them as they left, turning several locks as they went.

Fighting the reaction that had crept over her following the violence of the last few hours, Porcha wanted to curl up in a ball and let the world pass her by. But sleep was a luxury she couldn't afford. She needed to prepare herself to fight back. If she couldn't use Raul's weaknesses to her advantage then she might as well cut her own throat right here and now, because one thing was certain. Even if she did possess the information this Sanchez-Punto wanted, the moment he got it out of her, she'd be dead.

* * * *

The guys arrived at South Beach half an hour ahead of schedule. They scoped the area out but couldn't see anyone that didn't look like they belonged. Skaters, dog walkers, babes in miniscule bikinis, posers, grifters, the loud music that accompanied cocktail hour—welcome to Miami.

"It's hard to be sure if anything's off," Beck complained. "Everyone down here dresses like a wannabe gangster."

"Except the real deal, presumably," Adam suggested, mildly amused.

As satisfied as they could be that the area was clean, Troy took a conspicuous table at the outdoor bar they'd agreed upon as a meeting place. Adam and Beck were situated within sight of Troy and could see in both directions down the street.

"He's here," Adam said into his wrist mike ten minutes ahead of time. "Just three of them, far as I can make out."

"Let them get closer and then intercept," Troy said. "Beck, stay on the other end of the street, just in case they have reinforcements coming that way."

"You got it."

"He's limping quite badly," Adam informed the others.

Beck glowered. "Not as badly as he will be if he hurts Porcha."

"Okay, I see him," Troy said. "Go introduce yourself, Adam."

A short time later, Adam joined Troy, the three newcomers in tow. Troy stood up as they approached, sizing them up. Woollard had been beaten pretty good, and quite recently. His face was a mass of bruises, and Adam had been right about the limp.

"Woollard?"

"Yes, and you are?"

"Anderson. This is Cole."

"This is Kevin—"

Troy quirked a brow. "Mrs. Gonzalez's driver?"

"One of them." Woollard mangled his lips, as though he'd just been reminded of something unpleasant. "Mind if I sit down?"

"Are we gonna play nice?" Troy asked, pinioning him with a hard gaze.

"We're unarmed," Woollard said. "Search us if you don't believe me."

"We're *not* unarmed," Troy replied, indicating the seat opposite him. "Come on in, Beck," he said into his wrist. "You need to hear this."

"Damn right I do."

Beck joined them in seconds. Introductions dispensed with, they got down to business.

"I assume Georgio sent you to protect Porcha."

"Did he?" Troy folded his arms over his chest, waiting to see what else Woollard had to say before he gave anything away.

"Look, I don't know what she's told you about me, but you've probably got a distorted view. Believe it or not, I'm only trying to keep her alive."

"What happened to you?"

"I was with Sal when they got him." He indicated his battered face by waving a hand, also bruised, in front of it. "The rest of my body looks even worse, and I took a bullet in the thigh."

"But you got away and Sal didn't?"

"It wasn't me they wanted."

"How do we know you didn't kill Sal yourself, just so you could take over his operation *and* his wife?" Beck asked.

Woollard levelled an incredulous expression on each of them in turn.

"Why would I kill my own father?" he asked.

Chapter Seventeen

The goons had searched Porcha before they put her in the car. Her cell phone had been confiscated, but she had nothing else in her pockets for them to take. Raul, as she now knew him to be called—although she thought *goon* suited him better—had taken great delight in patting her down, but the fool had missed the lockpick and tiny device she'd shoved inside her bra. The ape was too busy feeling up the outside of her breasts to bother paying much attention to what was hidden in her cleavage.

"Idiots!" she muttered as she retrieved her treasures from their hiding place and set to work on the first of the locks.

"Damn!"

She threw the pick across the room half an hour later, with nothing more to show for her efforts than sore fingertips and a couple of broken nails to add to her scraped arms and aching jaw. The locks were more complicated than the ones she'd practiced her fledgling skills on back at the house, and she didn't have a prayer of cracking even one of them. She really should have insisted on taking the full course.

Porcha refused to admit defeat. If she couldn't open the locks from this side, she'd just have to wait until Raul came back and did so from his end. But then what? She needed a weapon. He knew she could take care of herself, and even he would have the sense to keep well out of range. She searched the small room, but there was nothing that wasn't nailed down that would help her. The bars on the window were firmly cemented in. The base of the bed was solid wood—no convenient springs for her to pry loose and fashion into weapons. The chair was flimsy plastic.

Frustrated, but still refusing to play the part of victim, she tried the toilet. An ordinary, smelly toilet and a wash basin. This was hopeless! About to give up, she felt a surge of excitement when she tested the toilet-roll holder. It was old-fashioned heavy metal.

And it was loose.

"Thank you!" she cried aloud, setting to work on the screws with her other tool.

It was painstaking work, but she had plenty of time and even more desperation to spur her on. It must have taken an hour, but eventually, with a cry of triumph, the metal fell away from the wall. She hefted it in her hand. If she could just take the guy by surprise, somehow catch him off guard, she might just be able to whack him with it. It wasn't heavy or jagged enough to do much damage on its own, but if she just got him off balance for a moment or two, she could possibly break a few of his limbs before she made a run for it.

But how to get him close enough to her to have a shot at it?

"Dumb question, Porcha."

She rolled her eyes. He was a man, wasn't he? She recalled the look in his horrible, piggy eyes when he patted her down, how he zeroed in on her tits when he cut her hands free. She almost chuckled as she threw off all her clothes.

"It hardly seems fair," she muttered as she placed her kit where it would be obvious if…when he opened the door. She left her bra and panties conspicuously on top on the pile, crawled under the blanket holding her precious weapon close to her side, and waited.

* * * *

"You're Sal's son?" Troy glared at Woollard, not believing a word of it.

"Yep."

"Porcha didn't mention it."

"She doesn't know."

"What, Porcha didn't know that her husband had a son older than she was?" Adam shared a sceptical look with the other two.

"Excuse us if I find that hard to believe," Beck chimed in.

"My mother was a Brit, like Porcha. Sal obviously went for classy English women. They weren't married, but Sal was mad about her, according to her, anyway. She fell pregnant about the same time she found out what Sal did for a living and what he was capable of, so she ran home to England and never saw him again."

"Did he know about you?"

"Not until eight years ago when Mom died. She told me about him but made me promise not to get in touch. She was convinced he'd want to control me if he knew he had a son, so out of respect for her, I didn't contact him until after she died."

"Did he believe you when you turned up on his doorstep claiming to be his long-lost son?"

Woollard rolled his eyes. "What do you think? Anyway, I told him who my mom was, showed him my birth certificate, and explained that I'd taken my mother's maiden name. It said 'father unknown,' but I think the dates got Sal thinking. Anyway, I offered to undergo DNA testing because I wanted to know for sure even if he didn't. He agreed, and it was a match."

Beck threw him a dirty look. "That must have made you very proud."

"He took me under his wing after that," Woollard said, shrugging off Beck's sarcasm. "He grilled me for hours about Mom's life after she left him, and he obviously didn't like what he heard."

"My heart bleeds," Adam muttered.

"We didn't have a lot, but Mom worked her butt off for what we did have, even though she could have made life a lot easier for herself if she'd wanted to. She was good looking, and tons of men were interested in her." Woollard shared a perplexed look between them. "I never understood why she didn't but always thought it was a case of once bitten and all that."

"Gonzalez never publicly acknowledged you," Troy pointed out.

"He didn't want anyone to know our true relationship because he was paranoid about people close to him getting kidnapped, or worse."

"Why were you so keen to meet him if your mom felt the way she did about him?"

"Like I said, Mom had standards. Unfortunately, that meant living in a rundown part of London and going without everything. Having a rich drug dealer for a father sounded quite sophisticated by comparison." He sighed. "It was a while before I realized Mom was right about him. I kinda respected him, but I could see just what a control freak he actually was. She said all along that if he'd known about me, he never would have given up until he had me with him. Same with her. I've often thought that's why he was so protective of Porcha. He'd lost the first love of his life. He wasn't taking any chances with the second."

"Informative as all this is," Troy said, actually believing it now, "we have more important things to worry about. Sanchez-Punto has Porcha."

"He thinks she knows where Sal's latest shipment of stones is," Woollard said. "Which is why I wanted to get hold of her before he did."

Troy raised an ironic brow. "You don't know where the stones are either, I take it."

"No, but—"

Beck fixed Woollard with a malevolent glare. "Sal loved her so much that he dropped her in it to save his own skin?"

"I can't even begin to think why he did that." Woollard shook his head. "He had some odd perversions that probably made Porcha hate him as much as she once loved him, but one thing's never been in doubt, at least not in my mind. He loved Porcha and would have died for her."

"Apparently not," Adam said.

"Kevin," Troy said. "There's one thing I don't understand—"

"Only one?"

Troy silenced Beck with a wave of one hand. "Mrs. Gonzalez said you drove her back to the Jupiter house, saw a gunfight going on, and got right on out of there. What was that all about?"

"That was me," Woollard answered for him. "Sal went to Mexico to sell out his drugs business to a rival. He'd promised Porcha he'd get out when he married her and had gradually been doing just that, but these things take time. We were there to finalize everything in person."

"So why Jupiter's answer to the OK Corral?"

"I'm getting to that. His greatest rival, and enemy, was Sanchez-Punto. They have a long history. Anyway, Sal wouldn't even think of selling to him, but he got word that Sal and I would be in Mexico City, and they were waiting for us. But they didn't care about drugs—"

"They wanted the diamonds," Troy finished for him.

"Right. They ambushed us, which was only possible because we'd been sold out by a person, or people, we trusted. Fernandez, the guy Sal did sell out to, got to us, but it was too late for Sal. He got me back to the States pronto so I could find out who'd turned on us. I was pretty badly bashed up, but I needed to be here, which is one of the reasons why I couldn't come looking for Porcha right away. Anyway, we surprised the guards, and the two guilty parties opened the gates and tried to make a run for it."

"Which is what we almost drove in on," Kevin added.

"Unfortunately, we didn't get them all," Woollard said.

"Let me guess." Troy rubbed his jaw with one hand. "Your fellow driver, Kevin?"

"Yeah," Woollard said. "Trevor had been with Sal for twenty years, and the bastard did the dirty on us." Woollard's head shot up. "But how did you figure that out?"

"They traced Kevin and Porcha to the hotel they checked into. I thought it was you, to be honest, and that you'd used a tracking device." He shrugged. "Process of elimination."

"Yeah, well, I knew about the apartment in Tampa and stupidly sent Trevor to see if Porcha was there. He must have told his new best friends, but presumably, you got to her first." Woollard breathed deeply. "Thank God for that."

"Where will they be holding her?" Troy asked.

"Almost certainly in his warehouse. He has one on the waterfront. Sanchez-Punto is an out-and-out family man, and he'd never take a hostage into his home and have his family exposed to the sordid side of his working life."

"He must have other properties."

"Yeah, but I still think the warehouse is where she'll be, at least overnight."

"Let's go," Troy said.

* * * *

Incredible as it seemed, Porcha must have dozed. She'd waited several hours for Raul to return, not daring to get out of bed because sod's law said he'd come back at the one time she wasn't ready for him. Then, of all things, she fell asleep. Her life was on the line and she was sleeping?

The sound of heavy footsteps on the tiled floor outside her prison woke her. Before she heard keys jangling in the locks she started moaning loud enough to wake the dead. The door opened just a couple of inches, and the barrel of a gun appeared round it.

"Where are you, bitch?"

"Argh, that hurts!"

Porcha brought her knees up to her chest and hugged them with her battered arms, writhing and whimpering when she sensed that Raul's head had now followed the gun barrel round the door.

"What are you trying to pull now?"

"I think I cracked a rib or something when you jumped me on the street." She writhed a little more, deliberately letting the blanket slip from her shoulder to reveal the side of one breast. "It hurts so bad I couldn't stand the restriction of clothing."

"I need you to stand up right now."

"Do I look like I can stand up? I'm in serious pain here. If you want me upright, you'll have to help me."

"Why the hell should I?" But he'd taken a step into the room, leaving the door open behind him as he eyed up her naked breast. "You're nothing but trouble."

"I think something's ruptured inside. I can't bear it. I—" She threw back the cover to reveal her naked body. "Please! Your boss wants me alive, but something's seriously wrong." Porcha forced out a few tears. "I think I passed out once already because of the pain, and I can't—"

"Where does it hurt?"

"My belly." She rolled onto her back, keeping her knees drawn up, and cried out when she touched her abdomen. He didn't appear to notice. Judging by the bulge in his pants, he had other ideas. "It's so painful. I can't stand it."

"You better not be faking."

"Do I look like I'm faking?" Porcha clutched her stomach and moaned even louder. "Just go away if you don't want to help me. I'm sure your boss won't blame you if I finish up in the hospital."

"Yeah, well, you won't be going nowhere 'cause Mr. Sanchez-Punto has had a change of plans. He's on his way to see you here right now, which is why you need to get up."

"Yeah, like that's gonna happen. Oh God, I think I'm bleeding."

That seemed to convince Raul to do something. He put the gun aside, leaned over her, and touched her stomach with one finger. "It hurts here?"

It was the best chance she was likely to get. As quick as a flash, she lifted her weapon and brought it down over his bent head with as much force as she could muster. He screamed as blood poured from a vicious-looking cut on the side of his head but had such a thick skull that he remained on his feet. Porcha didn't intend for that situation to continue. Whilst he staggered about clutching his head, blood seeping through his fingers, she leapt from the bed and took to the air. With both feet off the ground she made perfect contact with his neck, scissoring it between her feet. He landed heavily and finally lost consciousness.

Porcha didn't hang about, pretty sure he hadn't come alone. She pulled on her jeans and top without bothering with her underclothes. She threw her thong at the prostrate man, and it landed on his face.

"You were keen enough to get into my knickers, asshole, so knock yourself out." She let out an almost hysterical giggle. "Oh sorry, I already took care of that part, didn't I?"

She grabbed his gun. It felt heavy and unfamiliar but was hopefully loaded. Pausing only to check on the safety and how to remove it, she cautiously peered round the open door. Damn, Raul was moaning. She would like to take the time to find his cell phone but didn't dare risk it. It wouldn't take him long to come round, and, much as she disliked him, she didn't really want to do him further harm.

Unless she had to.

She slipped from the room and could see someone pacing up and down outside the street door, directly beneath an outside light. He was smoking and didn't seem to be particularly alert. He also didn't seem to be wondering what was keeping Raul, presumably because Raul had intended to deliver more than just food to Porcha.

Their thinking they could get away with abusing her lent Porcha fresh determination. She waited until the guard had paced as far away from the light as he ever seemed to, opened the door, and stepped out, keeping to the shadow outside of the light's range. Unfortunately, the door didn't close quietly and alerted the guard.

"That was quick," he said, grinning. "Hey, what the—"

Porcha now had no choice. He'd seen her and couldn't let her go. She had to act whilst she still had him off guard. Whilst he was still reaching for his gun, she flicked off the safety on her own, aimed for the guy's shoulder, and pulled the trigger. The gun felt heavy and unfamiliar and jerked upward when she fired her shot. He yelled and fell to the ground, clutching his arm. Her aim had been off. She suspected she'd only winged him, but it was enough to give her a brief advantage.

In full survival mode, Porcha saw headlights turn the corner and took off running in the opposite direction.

* * * *

Woollard was in the truck with the guys, directing Beck on the quickest route. It was midevening, but Miami traffic was as clogged up as ever, causing all four men to fume with frustration.

"It's up ahead," Woollard finally said as they turned the corner.

"What the fuck?" Troy peered through the windshield. "Who's that running away? I'd swear that was Porcha."

"It is," Beck said, putting his foot down, "and she thinks we're the bad guys."

A car came from the opposite direction, and Porcha was caught like a rabbit in both sets of headlights. In the moment she took to hesitate, Troy and Adam both leapt from the still-moving truck, calling her name. She snapped her head in their direction. It finally appeared to register with her who they were, and she ran full tilt toward them. At the same time, several people spilled from the other car, firing at them.

"Quick!"

Troy grabbed Porcha and thrust her at Adam. "Get her in the truck. I'll cover you."

Adam and Porcha ran. Troy walked backward, crouched low, returning the heavy fire being directed his way.

"Troy!"

It was Porcha's voice. He instinctively turned to see what was wrong, felt a searing pain in his right shoulder, and crumpled to the floor.

"Go!" he managed to shout to Adam. "Get her out of here."

Chapter Eighteen

"No!" Porcha struggled frantically to get free of Adam, but he picked her up and bodily carried her to the truck. As soon as he threw her in the back, Beck burned rubber.

"Troy!" Porcha wrenched her arms free from Adam's vicelike grip and hung her head out of the window. "You have to stop!" she yelled when Adam dragged her back into the truck. "Troy's hurt."

"Standard procedure," Beck said tersely. "We save you, not him. He'd do the same if it was between one of us and a hostage."

Porcha tried to argue, but the truck was already leaving the scene, taking the corner with a screech of tires. She saw a man of stature, presumably Sanchez-Punto, staring at her as she leaned out of the window. He was surrounded by men with guns, but none of them fired. Instead, they circled the prostrate Troy, weapons trained on him.

"They're going to kill him!" she screamed, bashing her clenched fists against Adam's chest. "Don't you care?"

"We care." Adam's jawline was rigid. "But I don't think they'll kill him. If they were going to do that, they wouldn't have waited."

"He's talking to the guy who led the team that broke into our place," Beck said. "I recognize him from the camera shots we got. Whatever the guy said, he's gesticulating toward you, and that prevented Troy being shot."

"Did you say anything to anyone about Troy?" Woollard asked from the passenger seat.

Porcha stiffened, only just noticing he was there. "What's he doing here?"

"Be glad that he is," Adam advised her. "Without him we wouldn't have found you in time."

"I—I blurted out Troy's name," she admitted.

The back of Beck's neck, which was all Porcha could see of him, went rigid. "They think you care about him?"

"I *do* care about him."

"Then you probably saved his life."

Porcha noticed Adam and Beck exchange a speaking glance, and there was a slight lessening in the tension between them. "How do you figure that one?"

"They'll offer him back to us in exchange for the information you have."

Porcha threw her hands in the air. "But I don't have it. Don't you think I'd tell them if I did?"

"No, but it gives us something to work with." Beck slowed down to the speed limit now they were clear of danger. "And it gives Troy a chance to find a way out."

"There isn't one."

"You managed it."

She felt tears seeping from the corners of her eyes. "I hadn't just been shot."

"I doubt whether they'll take Troy to the warehouse," Woollard said. "Because we know about it and because different rules apply to male prisoners."

"Damn." Adam thumped his fist against the side of the truck. "This whole fucking mission has gone to hell in a handbasket." He pulled Porcha against him, and she appreciated the support of his arm circling her shoulders. "How did you get away from them?" he asked.

Beck and Woollard both chuckled when she explained. Adam kissed the top of her head.

"Way to go," he said gently. "Don't worry about Troy. It'll take more than a shot to the shoulder to finish him off. Tougher people than these guys have tried to do away with him, but he's still breathing."

But Porcha could sense that Beck and Adam were both more worried than they were letting on.

"What happens now?" she asked.

"We go back to Jupiter, get you cleaned up, and see if we can think of a way to get him back," Beck said.

Porcha wanted to advise against trusting Woollard but held her tongue, and the rest of the journey was made in taut silence. When they arrived at the house, Adam and Beck accompanied Porcha to the master suite she'd shared with Sal and helped her into the shower. Once she was clean, Beck went to work with antiseptic lotion, gently cleaning up her scrapes and bruises.

"What happened to your face?" he asked.

"Raul hit me when I tried to get away from him in St. Pete."

"He's a dead man." Beck's chilling tone left no room for doubt on that score.

"I want to know about Woollard," she said once they'd patched her up.

"You ought to eat something."

"As if I could do that when they have Troy and it's all my fault." Fresh tears threatened. What was wrong with her? She never cried. "What happens now?"

"We wait," Beck said. "And we try to figure out where they might be holding him. Georgio's doing some digging for us."

"You need to hear what Woollard has to say," Adam told her. "If you feel up to it."

Porcha didn't want to go anywhere near the creep, but if the guys thought it was necessary, she trusted them enough not to argue.

"Okay, let's do it," she said.

Settled in the family room, Adam and Beck flanking her on a sofa, Woollard and Kevin opposite, Porcha listened to Woollard's story with growing disbelief. She wanted to scream that it was all a whopping great lie but already knew that it couldn't be. There had always been something special about Sal's relationship with Woollard, his inability to see the black side of his character, and now she knew what it was. Sal had desperately wanted a son, and it appeared the first love of his life had provided him with one who made him proud.

"Why did you..." Porcha gulped and tried again. "Why did you...I thought you wanted me to—"

"I hated that aspect of his life," Woollard said, "but it was the one area in which I couldn't influence him." He leveled his eyes on Porcha's face. "I know what you thought. You thought I wanted you for myself, but what you actually saw in my expression was disgust. I hated what he forced me to do to you, and I hated myself more for the way I reacted."

Porcha shook her head, not ready to accept that. "But you didn't mind the drugs and all the other stuff that—"

"Actually, I did." Woollard stretched his long legs in front of him and crossed them at the ankles. "At first, I thought it was all very glamorous, but after a couple of years of constantly watching my back, doubting everyone, living life in a gilded prison, I started to have doubts. I spoke to Sal about it, asked him how he could bear it, and do you know what he said?"

Porcha shook her head, intrigued in spite of herself.

"He said that he had nothing better to do with his time." Woollard half smiled. "Then you came along. He hadn't been serious about any woman since my mother, but I could see that he was totally gone on you."

Porcha tossed her head and blew air through her lips. "That's one way of putting it."

"He'd already promised you that he'd get out of the drugs game, and I knew he'd follow through. That's why he changed tack, and apart from building up his legitimate businesses, he also diversified into diamonds."

"He didn't need to do that."

"No, but I always knew going straight was going to take time for Sal. It was an alien concept for a lifetime criminal, but diamonds were a damned sight easier to move than drugs and, for someone with Sal's connections, far safer."

"Depends on your point of view," Adam said, a bitter twist to his lips.

"After that attack on you three months ago—"

"What attack?" Beck and Adam asked, turning toward her at the same time.

"Kevin got us out of it," Porcha said, flashing a smile at her former driver. "If what you say about Trevor is true, he probably told the bad guys where we'd be that day. Anyway, no harm was done, just a few bullets flying, but they all missed us thanks to Kevin's quick thinking."

"But Sal was really shaken up by it," Woollard said, "which is when he decided to quit procrastinating and get out of the drugs business once and for all. He could have tried to find out who was responsible, but he knew it would be a spiral that never ended, with constant tit-for-tat hits. I think he was tired of it all himself by then, and the hit on you was a wake-up call." Woollard stretched his arms above his head and sighed. "That's when he decided to sell out his drugs business *and* get out of diamond smuggling, too, so you could live a more natural life."

Porcha grunted. "Hardly that."

"He was to do one more extra-large diamond heist, and that would be it. From then on he would be an upstanding legal businessman."

"If you knew about everything he did," Beck said, "how come you didn't know how he was getting this last lot of diamonds in?"

"I'd been in Mexico for a while setting up the final meeting with Fernandez's people. When I got back he said it was all organized and I didn't need to be involved."

"How did he usually get them in?"

"He imports South African artifacts for resale here in the States. Wooden carvings, tapestries, stuff like that. Needless to say, he had all sorts of people in his pocket, principally a guy high up in the port authority. That ensured that any shipments in received only a cursory once-over. If there was a plan to do a more thorough search, Sal was always advised in advance and nothing was ever found."

"So we could, if necessary, direct Sanchez-Punto to the port authority guy?" Beck suggested. "That might get him off our backs."

"Possibly."

Adam pinched the bridge of his nose. "Why is Sanchez-Punto so set against Sal?"

"Ah, that's the thousand-dollar question." Woollard threw back his head and closed his eyes. "They grew up together as runners for the same drugs dealer and were great friends, until Sanchez-Punto fell in love."

Adam held up a hand. "I think I see where you're going with this," he said. "Sanchez-Punto fell for your mother, and Sal stole her from him. Am I right?"

"Spot on. I told you my mom attracted men. Sanchez-Punto worshipped the ground she walked on and has spent all these years waiting for the right moment to get his revenge by ruining Sal."

* * * *

Troy painfully regained consciousness when the car he'd been bundled into hit a pothole.

"Shit!"

He clutched his wounded arm and felt warm blood trickling through his fingers. The driver and his passenger didn't hear his muttered oath and carried on talking amongst themselves in Spanish. Troy understood every word.

"How the hell did this happen?" the passenger—presumably Sanchez-Punto—fumed. "How hard can it be to hold onto one woman?"

"I don't know," the driver responded. "Raul has a massive cut on the side of his head, and David has been shot."

Sanchez-Punto threw his hands in the air, looking ready to explode. "She took Raul's gun?"

Troy, in spite of the pain he was in, wanted to applaud. Never had he admired Porcha more.

"Yes, it seems she tricked him."

Sanchez-Punto let rip with a prolonged string of curses. "I'm surrounded by a bunch of incompetent idiots." Only Sanchez-Punto's heavy breathing broke the uneasy silence. "Why do you think we should keep this character alive?" he asked, hoisting a thumb in Troy's direction.

"The woman mentioned his name several times. She obviously cares about him. Perhaps we can trade him for the information we need?"

Sanchez-Punto grunted. "I'll think about it, but I wouldn't have to if you guys had shown one ounce of professionalism. What the fuck do I pay you so well for?"

The car drew to a halt in a seedy residential area. Troy's door was opened, and an arm yanked him to his feet.

"Argh, steady."

"Think yourself lucky you're useful to us, otherwise you wouldn't be worried about a pissing little flesh wound."

"Easy for you to say. It isn't your flesh."

Troy was marched through the house. From the brief glimpse he managed, it appeared to be occupied by a bunch of Sanchez-Punto's guards. Presumably, he didn't have a place here like Sal's with electronic gates and accommodation for the guards on the grounds. He took that to be a positive sign as he was led up the stairs to a small room on the upper floor. There was absolutely nothing in it.

"I need something to stop the bleeding," Troy said, still clutching his arm.

A couple of packaged military field dressings were thrown at him before the door was closed and locked. Troy had no water to wash the blood off or clean the wound up, but at least they'd left him to his own devices and weren't inflicting any further injury on him. At least not yet. As far as he could tell, it *was* just a flesh would. The bullet had gone straight through the fleshy part of his upper arm. He could see the exit wound. It hurt like hell, and would need sutures, but didn't appear to have done any lasting damage. He didn't need to be told that he'd been lucky. He slapped a dressing on it, awkwardly because he had to use his left hand, hoping that the wound wouldn't get infected.

After that Troy assessed his surroundings and was confronted by a barred window and a locked door. *Great, just great!* He looked up. The only outlet was a grid covering a utilities duct. Troy sighed. It looked as though he was going to have to do this the hard way.

He, too, carried a useful little gadget similar to the one that Porcha had used to effect her escape. His was sewn into a seam in his pants and had been missed when they frisked him. He extracted it from its hiding place and set to work on the screws that held the grid in place. He had nothing to stand on and could only just reach it by stretching up. Using his injured right arm was out of the question, and it felt awkward trying to prise loose tight screws without the right tool, using the wrong hand, and not being able to exert enough pressure from below. Still, what else was there to do to pass the time?

All the time he worked he thanked every deity he could name for Porcha's safety. The unbelievable had happened. He'd fallen deeply and passionately in love with the feisty Englishwoman and would give his life without a second thought if it meant she remained safe.

But she wasn't safe, he reminded himself, applying himself to the task in hand with renewed vigour. For reasons that escaped Troy, Sanchez-Punto was resolutely determined to find Sal's diamonds and wasn't letting anything stand in his way. Even if Troy got out of this, Porcha would never be safe until they either located the stones or neutralized Sanchez-Punto.

It took almost two hours of painstaking labor, but finally the grid fell free. Troy caught it before it could hit the floor, his good arm now aching almost as much as the injured one. *Okay, now for the hard part.* He had to haul himself one armed into that narrow space, crawl through it, and hope like hell that the other end didn't come out in the guards' main room. That would be just his luck.

Troy was grateful for all those hours spent in the gym when he managed to pull himself up at the first attempt with relative ease. The only problem was that the space was crowded with electric cables and air-conditioning paraphernalia, leaving little or no space for a man of his size—especially a man nursing an injury—to crawl.

With a deep sigh, he set about it anyway. He'd come through worse situations than this one, and no way was he beaten yet. He couldn't see a thing in the dark, confined space and had to feel his way with his good hand. It was impossible to protect his injured arm as he crawled along on his belly, ripping his skin on the rough rafters and protruding nailheads as he went. At one stage, he banged his injury so hard against a misaligned beam that he almost passed out from the pain. He cursed when he felt fresh blood seeping through the dressing but concentrated on the task in hand—on surviving.

At last he could detect faint light coming literally from the end of the tunnel. The fact that it was an electric light wasn't good news. It meant he'd emerge in a room that was in use. If it was permanently occupied then he was fucked, because it could only be a matter of time before he was missed, and even these idiots wouldn't have too much trouble figuring out where he had to be.

The end of the tunnel was covered by another grid. If this one was screwed down as well then he might as well admit defeat. He peered through the grating and found it came out into a bathroom. It was currently unoccupied but had to be in fairly frequent use or the light wouldn't have been left on. He could hear voices coming from a nearby room and the slap of cards against a wooden table. The guards were amusing themselves and not bothering to check on him. At last something had gone right.

Troy cautiously tested the grating by awkwardly twisting himself round in the slightly wider space at the end of the tunnel and pushing it with his feet. Much to his relief, it shifted. Presumably the one in the room he'd been in had been screwed into place to prevent any unwilling guests such as himself from escaping.

Nice try, scumbags.

About to pull the grill sideways into the tunnel to prevent it from falling onto the tiled floor beneath, Troy froze with it midway out of its housing when a burly guy appeared in the bathroom below. Had he heard a noise and come to investigate? If he glanced up he wouldn't be able to avoid noticing that the grill was missing. Worse, Troy realized, a steady stream of blood was leaking from his arm and dripping onto the bathroom floor. He hastily inched his way back a little, hoping his body would soak up the blood and prevent anymore getting through. There was absolutely nothing else he could do to protect his position, other than to pray.

The guy peed for what seemed like an eternity, and Troy remained stock-still in his cramped hiding place, not moving so much as a muscle. Finally, he finished, zipped up, and left the bathroom. Fortunately, he wasn't into hygiene. If he'd paused to wash his hands, he would almost certainly have noticed the bloody floor behind him in the mirror.

Troy gave him a moment to get clear and then awkwardly lowered himself into the bathroom. He made more noise than he was comfortable with, but something seemed to have gone his way for once and no one came to investigate.

The bathroom led directly into an upstairs corridor. A room to the right obviously contained the card-playing guards. The door was ajar, and Troy was fairly confident he could get past it without being seen.

The problem was, how did he get out of the house? Presumably they'd left someone on guard downstairs.

Only one way to find out. Troy, feeling dehydrated and light-headed, crept stealthily along the corridor, pausing when he got to the door of the card room. He waited until a roar of laughter covered any noise he might make and slid past the door in one swift movement, expecting to be challenged at any moment.

His heart rate returned to a more normal rate when it didn't happen. He paused at the head of the stairs, listening for sounds from below, but all was quiet. He couldn't afford to linger in such an exposed place and cautiously made his way down, treading on the outside of the steps to avoid making them creak. There was only one light on in the hall and no signs of life. Troy was absolutely convinced that an alarm would sound if he opened the front door. Tough, because wasting time looking for an alternative exit wasn't an option, nor was searching for a weapon.

Feeling exposed and vulnerable, he stepped forward and slipped the bolts back on the door, at the same time turning the key. He slipped through it just as a blaring alarm sounded and ran as fast as he could into the black night.

He could hear his pursuers shouting and slamming through the door behind him. It was essential to put distance between himself and them. Unfortunately, Troy didn't know the area, but he kept as much as he could to narrow alleyways and dark spaces. He heard a car engine start but didn't delude himself into thinking that they'd only follow him by car. This crew—or one much like it—had already fucked up by losing Porcha. They must be aware that their boss was all out of patience with them and couldn't afford to let Troy escape.

He actually thought he'd shaken them off, until he caught a glimpse of one of them at the opposite end of the alley he was in. He prayed the guy would be too lazy to enter the narrow passageway. If he did, Troy was dead, because there was nowhere to run.

The guy entered the alley.

Troy didn't stop to think. There was a large Dumpster just to one side of him. He dove into it, ground his teeth as pain ricocheted through his arm, pulled trash over his head, and tried not to breathe.

Either the guy hadn't actually seen Troy in the alley or he was a complete moron. Either way, he didn't look inside the Dumpster. Sanchez-Punto really needed to take a closer look at the caliber of goons he employed. Troy gave it five minutes and hauled himself out, covered in his own blood and smelling like a sewer rat. Not that he gave a shit. He was alive, and that was all that counted.

When he considered it safe to do so, he drifted toward a bigger road, hoping to find a place where he could call for the cavalry. The few people he passed on foot gave him a wide berth, for which he was grateful. Unsure where he was heading, feeling weak from loss of blood, Troy staggered on until he noticed a brightly lit building directly ahead.

A hospital. *Wonderful!*

He worked his way around to the entrance to the emergency room and slipped into the crowded waiting area. In this situation, a man covered in blood wasn't quite so conspicuous. A few people twitched their noses as he passed them, but other than that, no one gave him a second glance.

He found what he was looking for on the corner of the reception desk. He kept out of the way of the harassed staff working the desk, gauging his moment. When their attention was temporarily diverted, he snatched the telephone receiver with his good hand and rang Adam's cell.

Chapter Nineteen

"I still find all this rather surreal," Porcha said, regarding Woollard with a little less hostility. "Someone should have said something."

"I know that." Woollard shrugged. "I thought you ought to be told, but Sal was having none of it."

"Even so, I—"

Porcha stopped talking when Adam's cell rang. He looked at the display but clearly didn't recognize the number. He answered it anyway, his entire body jerking to rigid attention when he heard who was on the other end.

"Troy. Where are you?" he asked.

Porcha gasped. "What's happening?"

"We told you he'd be all right," Beck said, grinning inanely.

"Hang in there, buddy," Adam said. "We're on our way."

"Where is he?" Porcha felt relief bubbling inside her. "Is he all right?"

Adam and Beck were already on their feet. "Miami," Adam said. "How long?"

"It's eighty miles," Beck told him. "I'll get us there in under an hour."

"I'm coming, too," Porcha insisted.

Adam looked as though he was about to argue, but in the end he simply nodded. "Okay, let's go."

"You need me to come?" Woollard asked.

"No, we've got it, but we'll come back here when we have Troy. We need to get this thing with Sanchez-Punto sorted."

"I'll be here. Good luck."

Adam programmed the name of the hospital into the GPS as Beck hit the highway. Porcha sat in the back, admiring the way *her* two guys rode to the rescue of their best buddy with professional competence and little need for dialogue. In spite of the mess they were in, she felt safe and protected just by being here with them. More than that, she felt cherished, appreciated, and loved. Yes, loved. She instinctively knew that either one of them would have done what Troy did and sacrificed themselves to ensure her safety, and not just because they were assigned to take care of her. Unless she missed her guess, their feelings had gone beyond professional integrity, as had hers for them.

She examined the backs of their heads, resisting the urge to reach out and touch them both. They had their minds set on rescuing Troy, and rightly so. They didn't need any distractions from her. Porcha breathed an inaudible sigh. How could she explain to all three of them that she would have done the same for them? There wasn't a shadow of doubt in her mind on that score, because she understood now what love really meant. Not the suffocating, restrictive sort of love that Sal had shown her and which was the only type she'd experienced until she met these three. What she felt for them went far deeper, was more intense and so absolutely right that it felt as though everything she'd done in her life up until that point had been leading up to this moment.

Call her greedy, but she loved all three of them with a deep passion that shouldn't have been possible given the short amount of time she'd known them. Besides, how could one woman love and want three men equally? Porcha had no idea, she simply did. Not that it really mattered. It wouldn't last much longer. Once they'd rescued Troy, she'd be able to return to England and get on with her life. They might have fond feelings for her and want to protect her, but she wasn't stupid enough to imagine that it would end any other way.

True to his word, Beck got them to Miami in fifty minutes without being pulled over for speeding. They circled the hospital's parking lot and found the entrance to the emergency room.

"I don't see him," Porcha said, peering anxiously round the large space.

"Don't worry," Beck said. "He'll know it's us."

There was one corner that was darker than the rest. Beck pulled up there and flashed his lights twice.

A crouched-over figure emerged from the shadows, and Porcha let out an involuntary gasp as Adam jumped out and went to Troy's aid. He looked seriously injured, and Porcha's hand went to the door handle. She was a trained nurse. She could help him.

"Stay where you are," Beck said sharply. "Adam's got him."

"But I can—"

"No, you can't. It's you they really want, remember. They might well be watching Troy, waiting for us and *you* to come for him."

"Sorry, I didn't think."

The back door opened, and Porcha repeated her earlier gasp as she observed Troy, battered and bloody, barely conscious. His terrible smell barely registered.

"Troy!" She grasped his hand, and he squeezed it.

"Hey, babe."

Adam threw a first-aid kit Porcha's way. "See what you can do for him." He climbed into the passenger seat, and Beck sped away.

"Just leave it," Troy said when Porcha tried to administer help. "Get me somewhere safe then we'll sort it. It's not terminal."

Porcha wasn't so sure, but Troy's eyelids were drooping, he was clearly exhausted, and she was so relieved to have him back that she didn't argue. As an ex-nurse, she was well aware of the restorative powers of sleep and supported his head on her shoulder for the duration of the trip back to Jupiter.

Beck drove just as fast on the return journey, and as soon as they arrived, Porcha marched Troy into the master suite, stripped off his clothes, and went to work on him. Adam picked up his stinky clothing and disposed of it. He and Beck then stood back and let her get on with it.

"This wound needs stitches," she said. "We should have stayed at that hospital."

"No hospital," they said in unison.

"They'd recognize it as a gunshot wound, which would mean police, dah-de-dah," Adam explained.

"You stitch it, babe," Troy said drowsily.

"But, I don't—I can't. You'd need an anesthetic."

"He's a big boy." Beck's grin told them that he was back to his old, irrepressible self. Even so, his cover was blown because, he'd made a poor job of disguising just how concerned he'd been about Troy, and Porcha would have fun later teasing him about that. "He can take it."

"Well, all right then, but don't blame me if you finish up with ugly scars on that gorgeous body of yours."

"Hey, you never tell me my body's gorgeous," Beck said, affecting hurt.

"Those who ask don't get."

Porcha set to work. Troy hissed a few times, but apart from that he showed no reaction at all as she stitched his flesh back together in two places. He was pale, pain was etched in his features, but he really was a tough guy. Once she was done, she wrapped plastic round his upper arm.

"I'm afraid you really do have to hit the shower before you can sleep," she told him. "You smell like you've been in a Dumpster."

"That would be because I have."

"It's not the smell that bothers me," she said, "but the dirt could lead to infection. You've got a load of small cuts on your abdomen."

"That's what crawling through ceiling ducts does to a person." Troy looked dead on his feet but gamely tried to stand up. Adam gave him a hand. "Come on then, nurse, lead me to the shower."

"I'll join you," she said, stripping off.

"Hey," Beck protested.

"He can't wash himself." Porcha smiled sweetly at Beck. "Would you like to give him a hand?"

"Point taken," he said, grinning as he stepped back.

"Hell no!" Troy said at the same time. "You think I'd trust him anywhere near my delicate regions?"

Porcha chuckled. "That's what I thought."

Naked, she guided Troy toward the huge shower stall and switched on the water. She soaped him all over, and Troy actually sighed with pleasure. Hot water and getting clean appeared to revive him. Feeling light-headed with relief that they were all safe, she impishly took her time soaping his genitalia with a large sponge, repeatedly wiping it back and forth across his balls.

"Porcha!" Troy placed a hand on her arm. "I don't want you to think I'm complaining, but I really don't think I could manage it right now."

She dropped the sponge, stood upright, and wrapped her arms carefully round his neck. "I thought I'd lost you, Troy," she said, her voice breaking as the emotion she'd been holding in check came pouring out faster than the water poured over their heads. "You put your life on the line for me and almost died."

"Hey," he said, wrapping his good arm round her waist. "That's what I do."

"No one's ever tried to protect me like that before. My brave husband actually tried to save his own miserable neck by dropping me in it."

"Ah, but if he hadn't, we wouldn't have met."

"Don't make light of this, Troy." She tapped a finger lightly against his chest. "I want you to know how much I appreciate what you've done."

Troy kissed her. "It's okay, babe. It's all over now, and we won't let anyone hurt you ever again."

Porcha didn't understand how he could make such a promise but didn't press the point.

"I love you, Troy," she said simply, dropping her head on his chest. "I don't know how it's happened, but I love you all."

"What, even Beck?"

"Of course."

"Well, we love you, too." He captured her lips in a drugging kiss. "Where have you been all our lives?"

Porcha pulled herself together. She had given way to temptation in a weak moment but couldn't afford to indulge her vulnerable side indefinitely.

"We need to get you into bed," she said, turning off the shower and reaching for a towel.

She dried him off and then herself, unwrapped the waterproof protector from his arm, dosed him with painkillers, and tucked him into bed. He appeared to fall asleep as soon as his head hit the pillow.

"I'll stay with him," Porcha said, heading for the opposite side of the bed, "just in case he needs me."

"We need you," Beck said, playing the fool again.

"Your time will come, big boy," she said, pausing to kiss both him and Adam before climbing in next to Troy.

* * * *

Troy woke with the dawn, feeling battered, bruised, and lucky to be alive. It had been a close one. He glanced at the sleeping Porcha and died a little inside. Had she told him that she loved him or was that just wishful thinking? Well of course it damned well was! Why would a classy lady like her want anything to do with a has-been soldier like him—like them? He ran a finger along her hip, and her eyes instantly flew open.

"Are you all right?" She leaned up on one elbow, her tits dangling below her, and reached out a hand to touch his brow. "What do you need?"

"You."

"Troy, you've been badly hurt."

"Hmm, I can think of a good way to make the pain go away."

"You're in pain. Where does it hurt?"

"Right here." He took her hand and guided it to his erection. "Think you can do anything about that swelling, nurse?"

"Well, I'm not sure. Perhaps it needs washing." She ran her tongue across her lips, making it clear what she intended to do the washing with. "What do you think?"

His chuckle sounded as lethal as he now felt. "You're the professional health caregiver, so I'll be guided by you."

"That's right, I am." She dropped a light kiss on his lips. "So you'd best place yourself in my hands."

"Now *there's* a prospect to conjure with."

Porcha slid down his body, obviously taking care not to touch his cuts and bruises, and took his prick in her mouth. His sharp intake of breath lent nothing to pain as she sucked him deeper, gently agitating his balls as her tongue went to work. Troy closed his eyes and let her do whatever the hell she liked with those magical lips of hers. He'd earned this one.

The door opened just as he bucked to a climax in her mouth.

"No need to ask how the patient's doing," Beck said cheerfully. "I found you some fresh clothes," he added. "Not that you appear to need any right now."

"Morning, Beck." Porcha lifted her head and wiped her lips with the back of her hand.

"Morning, darling." He bent to kiss her. "Is that all part of your bedside technique?"

"It's the first thing they teach you at English nursing school. Far cheaper than prescription drugs."

"I can vouch for its authenticity." Troy sat up and winced. "Damned arm's still stiff."

Beck grinned. "Unlike the rest of you."

A short time later, Porcha joined Adam and Beck in the kitchen. Adam had taken over and produced breakfast, which Woollard joined them for.

"Glad to see you're okay," he said to Troy, appearing to mean it.

Adam waved a fork at him. "Tell us how you got away."

Troy gave them an abbreviated version.

"Sanchez-Punto's guards aren't very vigilant," Beck observed.

"No, I wouldn't like to be in their shoes right now," Troy agreed. "First Porcha and then I got past them."

"What are we gonna do about him?" Adam asked. "He won't let up, and now he has us in his sights, too. He's obviously a guy with a long memory who knows how to bear a grudge."

"It would help if we had some idea how he intended to get this last load of diamonds in," Troy said.

"I wish I could help." Woollard spread his hands. "But I honestly don't have a clue."

The internal house phone rang. Woollard stood up to answer it, asked a few curt questions, and then told the caller to let the delivery through.

"I'd forgotten about that," he said, sitting back at the table.

"About what?" asked several voices.

"Sal was celebrating his return to the paths of legitimacy—"

"Not that he'd ever occupied them in the first place," Beck pointed out.

"Whatever, he was marking the occasion by buying Porcha a car. He wanted her to be able to go out alone and just have fun driving. The car was to be your birthday present," he added, glancing at her.

"It's your birthday?" Troy, Adam, and Beck asked together.

"Tomorrow."

"Let's go see what your perverted husband bought you."

They trouped outside in time to see a bright yellow Porsche 911 convertible come to a stop outside the front door. The delivery guy gave Woollard something to sign and disappeared into the car that had followed him in.

Troy shared a glance with his two buddies.

"Now we know what Sal was really trying to say," he said.

Woollard shook his head. "What do you mean?"

"The guy you captured who'd been in on the interrogation of Sal told you he kept repeating two words over and over, right?"

"Yes, *Porcha* and *hidden*."

"Exactly. He wasn't saying Porcha knew where the stones were hidden," Troy explained. "He didn't drop her in it at all. He was saying that they were hidden in the Porsche."

Porcha gasped. "I'm guessing you're right." She paused. "I'm glad."

Troy touched her shoulder. "Get the car into the garage," he said to Woollard. "If there are diamonds hidden anywhere in the bodywork it won't take Beck long to find them."

An hour later, Beck reported that the car was clean. "But there *was* something hidden in the door panels," he said, washing his hands to remove the grease from them as he spoke. "The screws had been put back in a hurry and hadn't been tightened up properly."

"Which doesn't help us much," Adam said gloomily.

"Oh, I don't know." Troy fell into a kitchen chair, and the others, including Woollard, joined him. "Do we know when that car arrived in the country?"

"It usually takes between one and two weeks to clear stuff through all the channels."

"So, Sal's tame port man would have nodded the car through before word of Sal's death hit the news."

"And once he knew he was dead, he reckoned to take a little look-see and helped himself," Beck added.

"That's how I see it."

"Then we're still back to square one," Porcha pointed out.

"Not necessarily." Troy turned toward Woollard. "Are you serious in that you only want to be involved with Sal's legitimate businesses?"

"They belong to Porcha now."

"I don't want anything to do with them." She flicked a half smile at Woollard. "Be my guest."

"We can talk about that later. If I run them then you deserve a cut of the profits, not to mention this house and all Sal's other assets."

"There's nothing to talk about. I shall leave here with a suitcase full of clothes and nothing more. You're his son. It's all yours. I intend to make a new start. I don't want a life that's built on the profits from other people's misery." Adam was seated beside Porcha, and she reached for his hand. "I should have listened to Georgio and given Sal a wide berth."

"Sal *was* trying to give you more freedom by going legitimate," Beck said.

"No, I'm sure he wasn't. He was very good at flamboyant gestures, but I would still have been as firmly under his control as ever. Woollard's mother escaped him, and he wasn't going to let that happen a second time." She expelled a long breath. "He had me well trained, and although I hated what he made me do, it was as though he'd got inside my head and I couldn't seem to fight against him."

Troy smiled across the table at her. "What I'm trying to say is that Sanchez-Punto wanted to muscle in on Sal's diamond-smuggling business. Well, we might not be able to give him the diamonds, but we can give him a list of all Sal's contacts, the people along the line who made it happen." He glanced at Woollard, who nodded in agreement. "We can also tell him who we think has the diamonds that were in the Porsche. It'll be up to him what he does about that."

"And we give him all that in return for leaving us alone."

Troy shrugged. "Why wouldn't he? He'll have gotten what he wants."

They talked it over for more than an hour, but no one could think of a better way to resolve the problem.

"Okay then," Troy said. "Let's do it."

Woollard dialed the appropriate number and handed the phone to Troy. He asked for Sanchez-Punto.

"Tell him I'm the guy who escaped through the air duct."

A sharp voice came on the line seconds later.

"You have some nerve."

"I also have a proposition for you."

"I'm listening."

"I'd prefer to do this in person."

"I'm sure you would, but why should I agree?"

"You want the diamonds, don't you?"

"You have them?"

"I know where they are."

"Very well."

They agreed to meet in the same place on South Beach where they'd met Woollard.

"We don't have to do this," Troy pointed out. "We're coming to you in good faith to bring an end to this mess. Don't make me regret that decision and don't let me see more than three of you."

"I understand," Sanchez-Punto said curtly. "It's not you I want, and I guarantee that no harm will come to you, during this meeting at any rate."

Troy hung up, aware that the code of conduct pursuant to villains meant he'd probably keep his word. Besides, he had to be dying of curiosity. Even so, Troy didn't intend to take any chances.

"Pack that suitcase, Porcha," he said sharply. "Whatever happens, we'll not be coming back here afterward."

"Okay, it won't take me long."

"I need weapons," Troy said to Woollard.

"What do you need?"

Once Troy was armed to his satisfaction, they made yet another trip into Miami in two cars. Porcha traveled in the truck with the three guys, and Woollard was with Kevin and a couple more of his men in a car immediately behind them.

Sanchez-Punto was already seated at a table outside the bar they'd agreed to meet at. The boss man who'd tried to kidnap Porcha was with him along with another guy. Adam and Beck took up flank positions across the road. Woollard's men did likewise, completely surrounding the place and not attempting to hide their presence from Sanchez-Punto. It was just Porcha, with Troy on one side of her and Woollard on the other, who joined the party.

"I don't think I caught your name," Sanchez-Punto said by way of greeting.

"That's because you don't need to know it."

"The woman called him Troy."

"A Greek warrior or a wooden horse? Which are you, I wonder."

"You want Sal's diamonds," Troy said, ignoring the other man's attempts to get beneath his defences, "but they're gone." He held up a hand to prevent Sanchez-Punto's protest and explained what had happened.

"Then who has them?"

"We think the port official who Sal paid to look the other way. He was bent, greedy, and knew Sal was dead..." Woollard's words trailed off, like it had to be obvious.

"What we're prepared to offer you," Troy told him, "are the names of everyone who helped Sal bring the stones in, right back to the source in Africa."

"Why would you do that?"

"Because I don't want anything to do with it," Porcha said, shuddering. "I want to be left alone to get on with my life. I'm done with looking over my shoulder."

"And you?" He cast a glance at Woollard. "You were Sal's protégé. Why would you sell out the most lucrative part of his business?"

"For my mother's sake," he said, maintaining eye contact with Sanchez-Punto. "She didn't approve, you see."

The Mexicans exchanged a smirk.

"Didn't have you pegged as a mommy's boy."

Woollard didn't rise to the bait. "I'm sure you remember Ava," he said calmly.

An angry hiss escaped Sanchez-Punto's lips. "You were Sal's son?" he asked slowly. "Ava's your mother?"

"Yes."

"I had no idea." He shook his head. "The possibility hadn't once occurred to me, but now that you mention it, I see a faint resemblance round the eyes." He paused, lost in some distant recollection. "How is your dear mother?"

"She died from a respiratory disease eight years ago."

"I'm sorry." And he looked as though he really was. "She was a remarkable lady."

"That she was."

"So," Troy said briskly. "Do we have a deal?"

Sanchez-Punto extended a hand across the table. "We have a deal."

"You might wanna tighten up on your security before you embark on this venture," Troy said, unable to resist having a dig. "To lose two of us in the same day smacks of inefficiency, if you ask me."

"How's Raul?" Porcha asked sweetly.

"He's got a damned sight more than a bash over the head to worry about right now. And that goes for all the others, too." The Mexican flexed his jaw. "I didn't think I needed to send my best team just to capture one helpless woman. My respects, Mrs. Gonzalez," he added, inclining his head. "You equipped yourself well."

Chapter Twenty

Half an hour later, the truck was on its way back to St. Pete. Troy sat in the back, holding Porcha's hand, weary yet too hyped up to sleep the four-hour journey away.

"Seems to me like we have a birthday party to plan," Beck remarked from behind the wheel. "What would you like from us, sweetheart?"

"Hmm, I get to choose, do I?" She plucked at her lower lip, as though thinking about it. "Well, in that case, how about I have you all?"

Troy grinned. "If you ask me, we've got an insatiable little sub on our hands."

"And that's a bad thing because…" Beck grinned at Troy and allowed his words to trail off.

"It's not my fault that I love you all and can't choose between you."

"For my part, I shall rise to the occasion in more senses than one and excel myself in the culinary department," Adam told them.

"You always do." Porcha leaned forward to kiss the back of his neck. "You'd make someone a lovely husband."

He flashed a grin over his shoulder. "You offering, babe?"

"No, she isn't," Beck answered for her.

"Have I told you guys how amazing you were back there?" Porcha asked. "All those risks you took for me were quite something, but then playing hardball with Sanchez-Punto at the end when you could have just left things in abeyance." She shook her head. "I haven't done anything to deserve such service."

Beck took one hand off the wheel, reached back, and patted her knee. "I wouldn't say that."

"I'm sure you'll find a way to express your thanks." Troy's hand crept across her thigh. Her legs fell open, giving him access to her crotch. He explored it with the pad of his thumb through the denim of her jeans. "We like surprises."

"Can I stay with you until I—"

"Where else would you stay?" all three of them asked together.

"Until what?" Adam asked suspiciously.

"Until I arrange a flight back to England, of course."

"Why would you want to do that?" Troy asked, perplexed.

"It's home," she said simply.

"Home is where the heart is, babe," Beck said.

She sighed. "If only it were that easy."

They arrived back at the house to find the door repaired and new keys awaiting them. Troy's desk had been replaced with a sound version of the same model and, significantly, no signs of the struggle that had gone down were now evident. The body had been removed, as had all blood traces, and everything was back in its place.

"Gotta love Georgio," Beck said.

It was late evening by then. Adam knocked together a simple meal, and as soon as it was over Porcha claimed fatigue and took herself off to bed.

"We have a problem," Troy said as soon as she'd gone. "We can't possibly let her to back to England."

"Damned right we can't," Beck agreed.

"I don't like it that she took herself off to bed alone," Troy said, scowling. "It's like she's already distancing herself from us."

"Would she stay with us if we asked her to?" Adam asked. "What can we offer her that she didn't have in greater abundance with her creep of a husband?"

"Three large cocks. Far as I can gather, she only ever got one there." Beck scowled. "*And* he humiliated her for sport, the bastard."

"She did say she loved us all," Troy reminded them.

"Yes, but she might not have meant it in the way you hope she did." Adam grimaced. "I reckon we need to give her what Sal didn't, and that's freedom to be herself. That way she'll enjoy submitting to us but will have a sense of self-worth, too."

"Yeah," Beck grumbled, "but how do we do that?"

"Okay." Troy nodded in agreement. "Tomorrow's her birthday. Here's what I suggest."

* * * *

Porcha woke early on the morning of her twenty-sixth birthday and stretched her arms above her head, feeling rested and restored. She smiled when she recalled where she was. She'd half expected one of the guys to join her during the night, but they were obviously as exhausted as she herself had felt. Still, this was a new day—her day—and she fully intended to enjoy them all to the full.

She jumped out of bed, hit the shower, and then wandered downstairs wearing shorts and a strappy top.

"Happy birthday!"

Three handsome faces grinned at her. The kitchen was festooned with heart-shaped balloons and there were fresh flowers on every available surface.

"Hmm, someone's been out shopping early." She gave each of them a hug and kiss in turn. "Thanks, guys."

"Okay," Troy said as soon as breakfast had been cleared away. "We're gonna hit the shops now."

They drove her to a local mall and raided Macy's. Over her protests, they purchased her what felt like an entire wardrobe, with definite emphasis on underclothes. She couldn't really understand why, because they seldom let her wear any when she was in the house, but she was having too much fun to argue with them.

"Just remember," Beck said, flashing an especially garish thong beneath her nose, "whenever you wear this, you're mine."

"I'm yours anyway, handsome," she said, standing on her toes so that she could aim a kiss at his lips.

"Hear that, losers," he said to the other two. "Porcha's all mine."

Adam rolled his eyes. "He does so enjoy his little delusions."

"Aw, Beck. Won't you share me with Troy and Adam?" she wheedled. "It'll be so much more fun that way."

Adam grinned. "Why settle for one cock when she can have three?"

"Precisely what I thought," Porcha said happily.

They had lunch together in the mall like a proper family, but as soon as they got back to the house the men dispersed. Beck headed for the gym, Troy for his computers, and Adam started preparing his birthday feast. Porcha, not wanting to cling, took herself off to her room and tried on some of her new outfits, wondering what to wear for her birthday dinner. Was the decision hers to make or would the guys would have their own ideas on the subject?

She must have dozed off, but delicious smells coming from below woke her. She pulled on a pretty bra-and-panty set that Adam had chosen, a simple shift dress in bright turquoise that Troy had picked out, and fastened on an expensive gold bracelet that Beck had insisted on buying her. She put on her collar, just in case they had any doubts about what she expected from them as her main present, ran a brush through her hair, and headed for the stairs.

She was greeted by a chorus of wolf whistles. Each guy in turn kissed her, and someone handed her a glass of champagne. She lowered her eyes, happy to fall into her submissive role as she waited to be told what to do next. Her new panties were already soaked through, and her heart raced with anticipation. Adam took her hand and led her to a chair. A single-occupancy chair. That was strange. One or more of them always wanted to sit with her. She felt the first stirrings of alarm. What was going on here? Surely they weren't going to tell her it was time for her to leave. Not on her birthday.

"We need to talk to you, Porcha," Troy said.

"Yes, master."

"No, we need to talk to you as you, not as our sub."

Her eyes snapped to his face. "What's wrong?"

"Absolutely nothing. We love having you here." He paused. "We haven't known you for long, but it's long enough to know that we love everything about you. In short, we all love you."

"Absolutely," Adam agreed.

"Never felt like this before," Beck added.

"And I love all of you."

"Then why go back to England?"

"Well…well, I have to go somewhere."

"You wouldn't consider staying here with us?"

Porcha opened her eyes very wide. "What, all of you?"

"You don't get what you want from us?" Adam asked, grinning.

"Yes, you know I do, but how can one woman keep all three of you—three virile men—satisfied indefinitely?"

"You've done a bang-up job so far," Beck told her.

"You're serious, aren't you?"

"Never more so," they said together.

"I know it's a lot to take in, and you probably think it's too soon after Sal to get involved in a serious relationship." Troy spread his hands. "We get that, and we're prepared to wait. You can stay with us on whatever basis you're comfortable with until you've had time to reach a decision."

"That's very generous, and a very tempting offer, but I—"

"We've talked about this," Troy said. "It's what we all want, but for you it won't be like with Sal. You'll submit to us in the house, but you can still be yourself, have a life of your own outside of it that we don't control."

"I don't see how." Porcha shook her head. "Tempting as it is to say I'll stay, you three will be dashing off on another job soon, leaving me to kick my heels up here because you don't want me to be endangered." She lifted her eyes to one dear face after another. "I love you all, but that's not enough. I *can* look after myself, and in case you don't believe me, I'd best remind you that four men broke in here. I killed one and didn't break down and go all girly when I saw the blood. I threw a second one across Troy's desk, *and* I gave the third one a good kick in the gonads before they took me."

Troy laughed. "Wish I'd known about that last part. I wouldn't have been able to help mentioning it to Sanchez-Punto yesterday if I had."

"See, you're making a joke out of it."

"No, love, I—"

"When I was captured I managed to escape, tricking one guy and shooting another in the process, and *you* want to protect *me*." She shook her head. "It wouldn't work."

"Which is why we're offering you a place on the team, if you want it," Troy said, smiling at her. "You didn't let me get to that part."

"You're what!"

"One of the many things we love about you is your courage," Beck told her. "Your feisty determination to fight, to give as good as you get, and the hell with the consequences."

"That aspect of your character is probably coming out so strong because Sal kept you so securely under his thumb," Adam added.

Beck nodded. "But we think we've seen the real you and, hey, we love what we see."

"We often get jobs that involve looking after a woman," Troy said. "Your inclusion in the team would help a lot there. Look how you reacted to us when we first called on you, but if there'd been a woman with us, I'm betting you'd have felt differently."

Porcha nodded, in a daze. They really seemed to be serious. "But there's a lot I don't know."

"Nothing that we can't teach you."

"I'm scared of the water, which is one of the reasons why I didn't run into the yard when those guys broke in. I had a bad experience in a swimming pool when I was a kid, and I never really got over it."

"We'll get you through that."

"What do you say, babe?" Troy asked. "Will you stay here to work and play with us and let us love you like you deserve to be loved?"

Was she crazy, even hesitating? They were offering her the sort of opportunity she'd never dared to even dream about. A job, a home, three hunky lovers…Any woman in her position would jump at the chance.

"I say yes!" She leapt up and flung her arms round Adam's neck, simply because he was the closest one to her.

"That would be yes, master." He disengaged her arms, and just before she dutifully dropped her eyes, she noticed the triumphant smile Adam shared with his two buddies. "Assume a submissive position, Porcha. We're not at work now."

"Yes, masters."

Porcha dropped to her knees in front of Adam. Happiness fizzed through her bloodstream as she told all three of them with her eyes and her body language that she didn't need to think about their proposition.

She was theirs for keeps.

THE END

WWW.ZARACHASE.COM

ABOUT THE AUTHOR

Zara Chase is a British author who spends a lot of her time travelling the world. Being a gypsy provides her with ample opportunities to scope out exotic locations for her stories. She likes to involve her heroines in her erotic novels in all sorts of dangerous situations—and not only with the hunky heroes whom they encounter along the way. Murder, blackmail, kidnapping, and fraud—to name just a few of life's most common crimes— make frequent appearances in her books, adding pace and excitement to her racy stories.

For all titles by Zara Chase, please visit
www.bookstrand.com/zara-chase

Siren Publishing, Inc.
www.SirenPublishing.com

Lightning Source UK Ltd.
Milton Keynes UK
UKOW031849250613

212811UK00017B/935/P